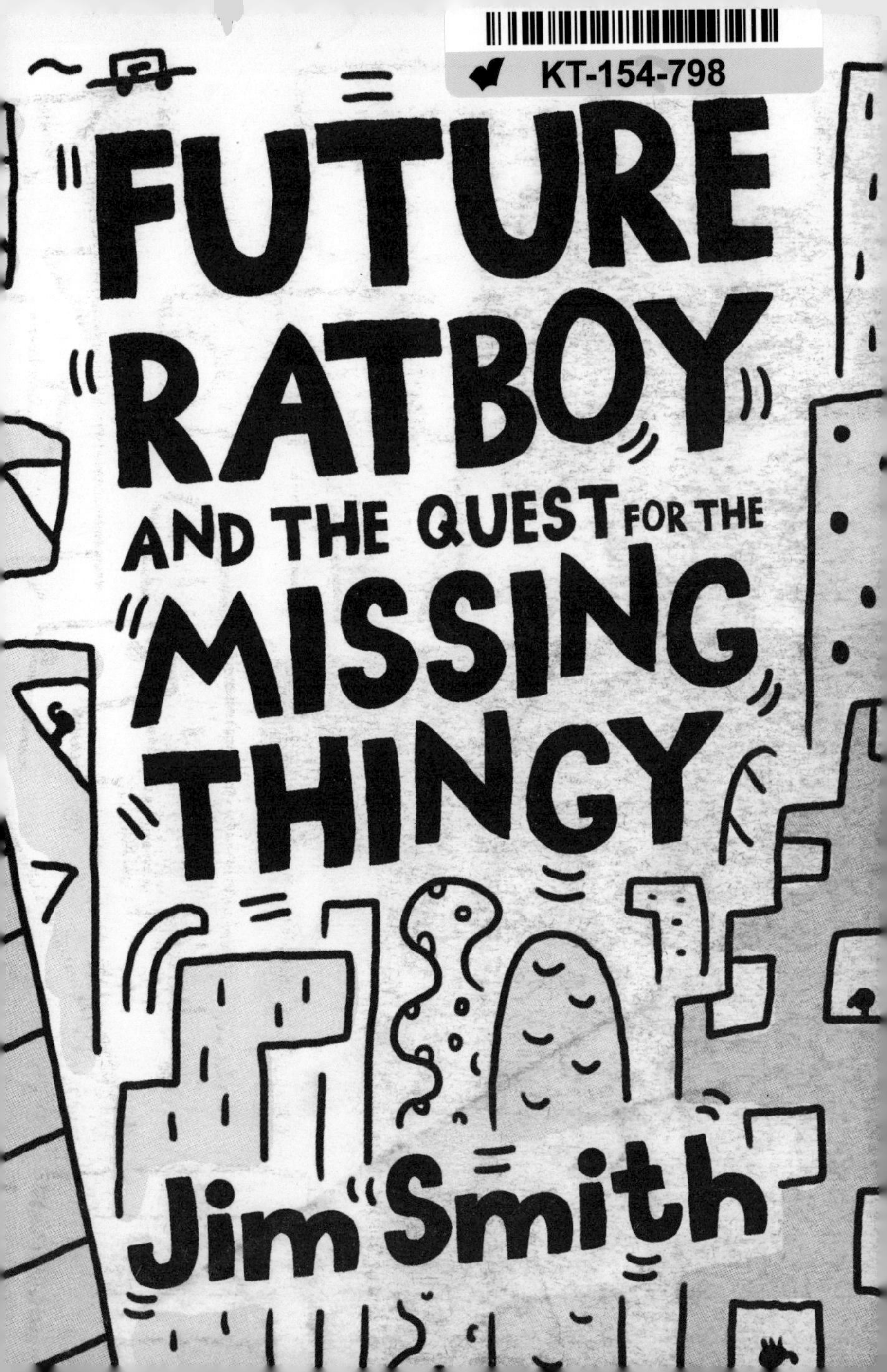
FUTURE
RATBOY
AND THE QUEST FOR THE
MISSING
THINGY
Jim Smith

"PRAISE FOR MY "OTHER" BOOKS

'Will make you laugh out loud, cringe and snigger, all at the same time'
-LoveReading4Kids

'WHAT'S NOT TO LOVE?'
-Sun

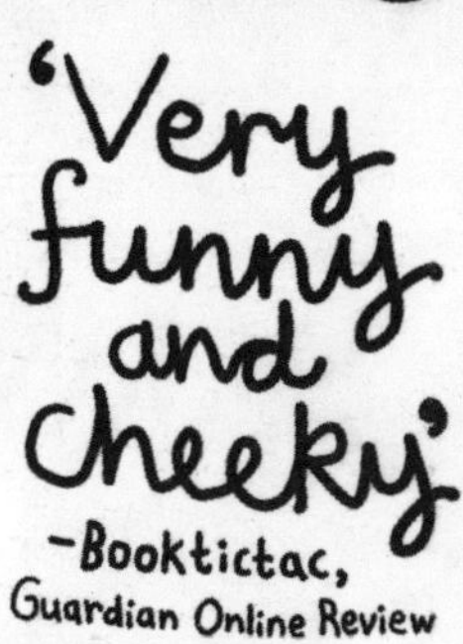

-Booktictac, Guardian Online Review

'I LAUGHED SO MUCH, I THOUGHT THAT I WAS GOING TO BURST!'
Finbar, aged 9

'The review of the eight year old boy in our house... "Can I keep it to give to a friend?" Best recommendation you can get' -Observer

'HUGELY ENJOYABLE, SUR
CH
-

I am still not a Loser
The Roald Dahl
FUNNY
E
013

EGMONT
We bring stories to life

First published in Great Britain 2017
by Egmont UK Ltd, The Yellow Building,
1 Nicholas Road, London W11 4AN

ISBN 978 1 4052 8398 4

www.futureratboy.com
www.egmont.co.uk

A CIP catalogue record for this title is available from the British Library

Printed and bound in Great Britain by the CPI Group

63323/1

PREVIOUSLY ON FUTURE RATBOY...

Hello, my name is Colin Lamppost. At least it used to be. Then one day me and my cuddly toy bird were inside a wheelie bin when it got hit by lightning.

We were zapped from our home town of Shnozville millions of years into the future and I was transformed into a half boy, half rat, half TV.

Future Ratboy was born.

Now I've got aerials sticking out of my head, a telly on my belly, a cape made out of a bin bag and a plug-tail hanging off my bum.

Oh yeah, and my cuddly toy bird got turned into a real-life bird.

He shouts 'NOT!' after everything I say.

HEY, NOT BIRD!

NOT!

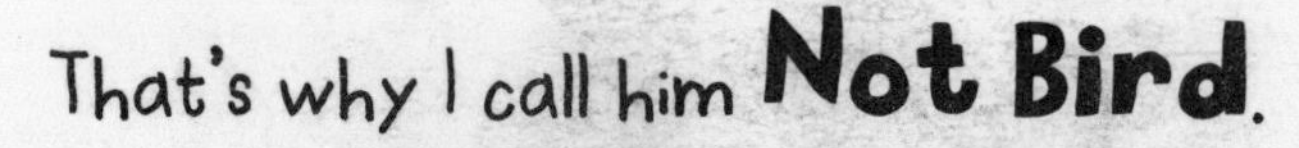

That's why I call him **Not Bird**.

Now we live with

Bunny,

the owner of Bunny Deli, the **keelest** burger shop in Future-Shnozville.

(**'Keel'** is how we say 'cool' in the future, by the way.)

Bunny Deli is also a sort of orphanage for children whose mums and dads aren't around.

Like **Jamjar**, whose mum and dad shrunk themselves to the size of full stops during a science experiment once.

Jamjar's got five arms and is really brainy.

Then there's **Twoface**,
who thinks he's a superhero like me.
His parents are too busy being
real-life superheroes to look
after him.

And **Splorg**

the blue-skinned alien.

Splorg's parents were eaten by a black hole when they went out to dinner one night.

This is **Mr X**.

He's the evil baddy who wants to take over Shnozville.

I've promised my friends I won't zap myself back home to the olden days until he's defeated.

And this is **Wheelie**, the bin I got zapped here inside.

Mr X fitted him with a speech module and gave him some arms and dressed him in a waiter's suit.

But that's another story.

At the end of the last episode, Mr X kidnapped our friend,

The Wise Old Vending Machine,

and we haven't seen either of them since.

Something tells me that's all about to change though . . .

I've been here in the future for a while now, but I'm still not completely used to it. Like the other day for example. It was the forty-ninth of Socktober and me and the gang were strolling into town for a very important occasion.

I looked up at the tree we were walking past and gasped. Hundreds of multi-coloured socks were dangling from the ends of its branches like, erm . . . socks.

'Sometimes I wonder if this whole being-in-the-future thing is all a weird dream!' I said. 'I mean - socks growing on trees? That's just ridikeelous!'

'NOT!' squawked Not Bird, flying over my head and perching on a branch. The whole thing swayed and a sock fell off, landing on Twoface's left face.

'What's so ridikeelous about it, Future RatLOSER?' said Twoface out of one of his mouths. He peeled the sock off his head and threw it on the pavement outside Dr Smell's perfume shop.

'Yeah Future RatBUM, it's just a plain old sock tree!' he said out of his other mouth.

Twoface has been calling me names like that ever since I won the Shnozville Superhero of the Month award for helping an old granny cross a road.

I know that doesn't sound like much, but the road was seventeen miles wide. And the granny was a ninety-four-year-old elephant. And I had to carry her. With one hand.

I think Twoface is just jealous because he reckons he's a better superhero than me.

The door to Dr Smell's perfume shop opened and Dr Smell stepped out. He sniffed the air then glanced down at the leaf sock Twoface had just thrown on the floor.

'Hey, I only just swept that hover-pavement!' he frowned. 'Blooming socks everywhere,' he said, picking the sock up and throwing it in a clear plastic hover-bin bag filled with eight trillion other leaf socks.

Jamjar pointed at the hover-bin bag and pushed her glasses up her nose. 'One of the keel things about living here in the future,' she said to me, 'is that nobody has to buy socks any more!'

'Amazekeels,' I said, even though I didn't have to buy socks when I lived in the olden days either, because my mum and dad always bought them for me.

'Heading into town are you, gang?' said Dr Smell, waggling his nostrils. 'I can smell excitement in the air!'

That's how good Dr Smell's sense of smell is - he can even smell excitement.

Wheelie flapped his lid open and shut, and Dr Smell stuck two of his fingers up his nostrils to stop the bin stink floating up them.

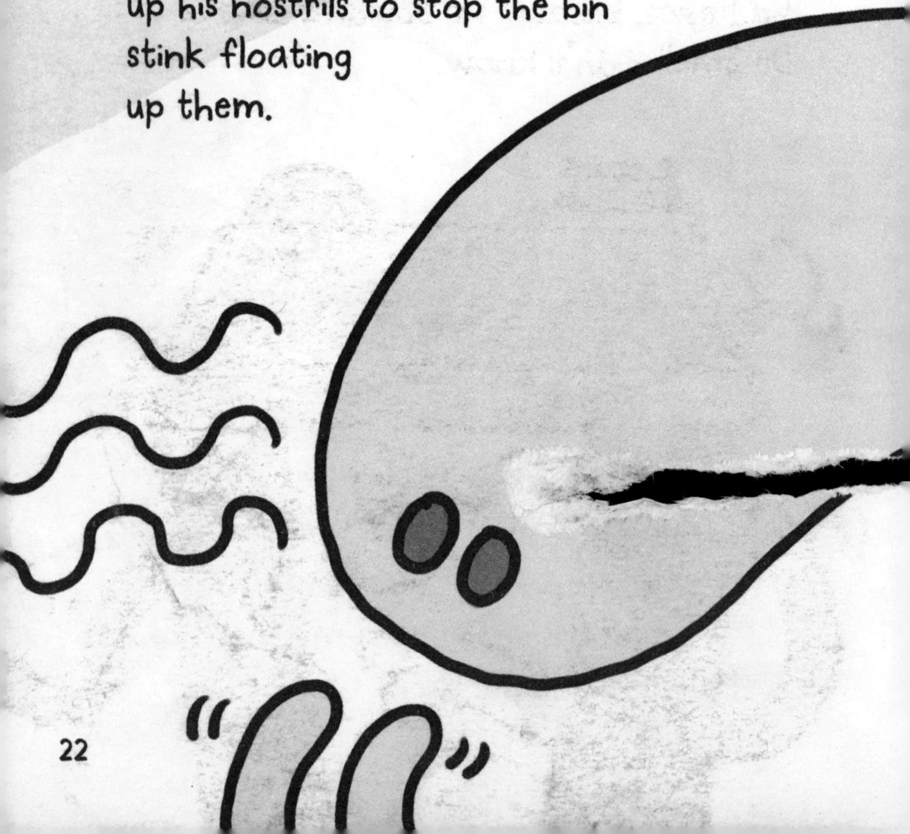

'OOH YES,' bleeped Wheelie in his posh new computery voice, and I thought how weird it was that my normal old bin from home could now speak. 'TODAY IS A MOST IMPORTANT DAY!'

'What's happening?' asked Dr Smell, and Wheelie rolled the bits of his lid where his eyes would've been if he'd had eyes, because he couldn't believe Dr Smell didn't know.

'WHY, IT'S MAYOR GOODHAIR'S BIRTHDAY, OF COURSE!'

burped Wheelie.

Dr Smell knocked on his head like it was a front door.

'Blistering bogazoids, I'd completely forgotten!' he said. 'Ratboy, isn't YOUR birthday coming up soon too?'

'Next week,' I said.

'NOT!'

squawked Not Bird, even though my birthday really was next week.

'Got anything planned?' asked Dr Smell.

'No,' I mumbled, imagining my mum and dad and little sister back home in the olden days, hanging bunting and crossing their fingers I'd turn up again one day at their front door.

'What, no party?' said Dr Smell, and I shook my head.

Twoface's two faces smiled to themselves. 'Old RatNOSE here is scared his bday bash wouldn't be as good as Mayor Goodhair's,' he sneered.

'No I'm not,' I said, and Not Bird squawked,

'It's true, the mayor's parties are hard to beat,' said Splorg. 'Free food and drink for everybody - plus he's unveiling a brand new statue of himself today at seven billion o'clock on the dot!'

Dr Smell twitched his nose. 'ANOTHER Mayor Goodhair statue?' he said. 'That's the 57th one this year!'

'You know Mayor Goodhair – he loves a statue of himself!' chuckled Jamjar, and I put my hand up, like I was in school.

'Erm, I don't want to sound stupid or anything, but can anyone tell me who Mayor Goodhair is exactly?' I asked.

'Mayor Goodhair is the mayor of Shnozville,' said Jamjar.

'Obviouskeely,' chuckled Twoface, and Not Bird did a sniggle.

Jamjar ignored Twoface. 'You know how Mr X goes round town blowing things up and causing trouble?' she said, and I nodded. 'Well the mayor is sort of the opposite of that - he replaces hover-pavements when they're broken and makes sure everything's clean and tidy.'

'And why is he called "Mayor GOODHAIR"? I asked.

Jamjar pointed across the road at a statue of a man with an extremely good head of hair. Underneath his head was a little brass plaque with writing on it.

I Future-Ratboy-zoomed my eyes in and read the words 'Mayor Goodhair'.

'Because he's got the keelest hair in the whole of Shnozville!' chuckled Dr Smell.

Haven't heard much about Mr X recently, have we?

said Twoface, as we waved goodbye to Dr Smell and carried on walking towards Shnozville Town Square. 'Ever since he kidnapped The Wise Old Vending Machine he's completely disappeared off the face of Shnozville!'

'Maybe I scared him off,' I smiled, pointing to myself. 'I am the Shnozville Superhero of the Month, after all!'

'NOT!' screeched Not Bird, and Twoface cackled.

Not Bird squawks 'NOT' after everything I say, in case you haven't noticed. And it's been really getting on my nerves recently.

'You do realise you're my sidekick, don't you, Not Bird?' I asked. 'That means you're sposed to be on my side.'

'NOT!' squawked Not Bird again, and I picked up a leaf sock off the pavement and thought about stuffing it into his mouth, just to shut him up.

Jamjar did her serious face. 'I wish Mr X WOULD disappear off the face of Shnozville,' she said. 'I've got a feeling he'll turn up again sooner or later, though.'

I dropped my leaf sock and put my arm round Jamjar. 'Don't worry, Jamjar. Future Ratboy will protect you from the evil Mr X!' I said in my keelest superhero voice.

'NOT!' screeched Not Bird for the seven trillionth time that morning. He high-fived Twoface with his wing and I felt the TV on my belly fizzle like a shaken-up can of Hedgehog Cola.

'I tell you what, Not Bird,' I snapped. 'Why don't you just be Twoface's sidekick? Because it's pretty obvious you don't want to be mine!'

'NOT!' screeched Not Bird, snuggling into Twoface's neck.

'NOT YOURSELF!' I shouted back.

'Ratboy! Not Bird!' cooed a familikeels voice, and Bunny appeared behind us, wobbling along the pavement to catch up.

'Stop bickering, you two!'

Splorg looked at Bunny like he'd never seen her outside of Bunny Deli before.

'What are YOU doing here?' he asked.

'I couldn't miss Mayor Goodhair's birthday party, could I?' smiled Bunny, looking round at us all. 'Ooh, you are a bunch of adorable little weirdos!' she giggled, giving us a cuddle each, which didn't take that long seeing as she's got ten arms.

I glanced over at Splorg with his shiny bald blue head, Jamjar with her five arms and Twoface with his two stupid faces.

They were definitely the strangest-looking friends I'd ever had.

'I wonder what Mayor Goodhair's gonna get for his birthday!' said Splorg, and I thought about my mum and dad again, wrapping up my present for next week.

Maybe, if I was lucky, Mr X really would disappear off the face of Shnozville. Then my work here in the future would be done and I could zap myself home in time for my birthday.

But how could I leave this lot?

It wasn't like I didn't have friends back in the old days. They just weren't quite as keel as these ones.

'What you looking so serious about, Ratbogies?' asked Twoface, snapping me out of my thought bubble.

'Nothing,' I said, as we turned the corner into Shnozville Town Square.

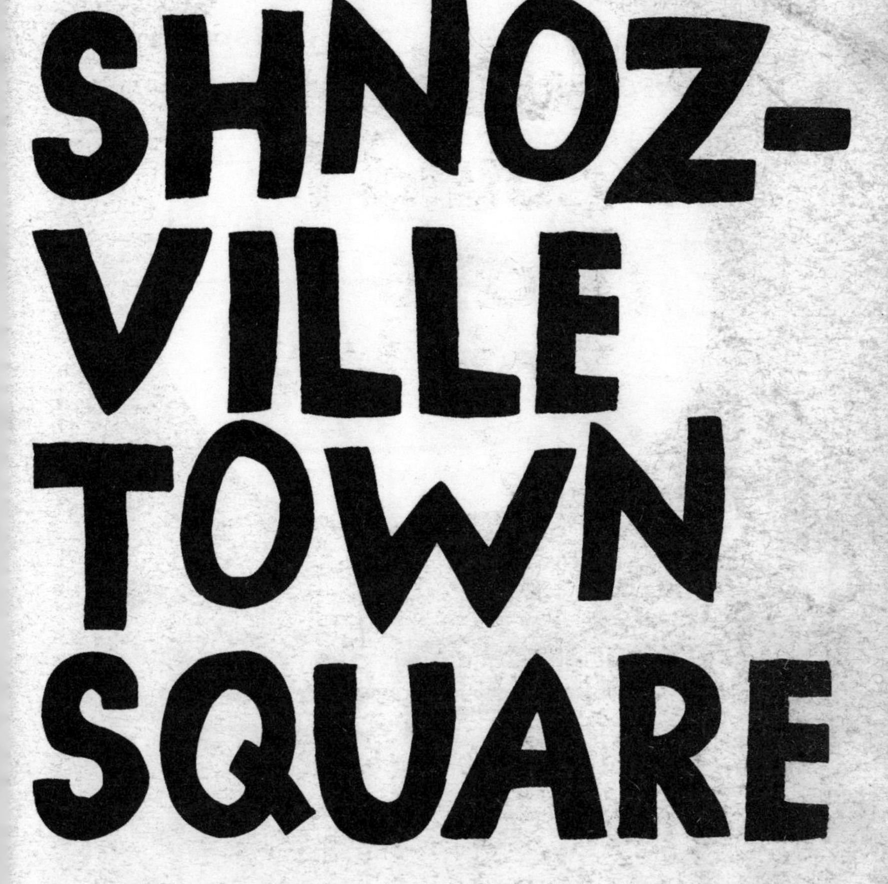

Slap bang in the middle of Shnozville Town Square stood what looked like a statue with a ginormous yellow sheet draped over it. Around it was tied a red ribbon.

Next to it hovered a parcel five times the height of a sock tree, wrapped in pink wrapping paper. Around this one was tied a yellow ribbon.

There were five other statues of Mayor Goodhair dotted round the square that I hadn't noticed before.

'You weren't kidding, Jamjar,' I said. 'Mayor Goodhair really does like a statue of himself!'

'NOT!' squawked Not Bird, but slightly quieter than usual, probably so Bunny wouldn't hear.

I looked at the giant presents. A massive crowd had gathered round them and hover-cameras zigzagged through the air, filming for Shnozville News.

'Good mornkeels and welcome to Shnozville News!' boomed a wrinkly old man on a huge hover-screen floating above my head. 'I'm Bill Aardvark and this is my co-host, Cecelia Twizzlefrump!'

The camera panned across to a blonde lady with three noses. 'We're live at the scene of Mayor Goodhair's nine hundred and seventy-twelfth birthday party!' she yakked, and a photo of Mayor Goodhair popped up behind her on the screen.

I Future-Ratboy-zoomed my eyes in on the photo. Dr Smell was right, Mayor Goodhair had the shiniest, bounciest hair I'd ever seen.

'You've got to love him, haven't you?' said Splorg, staring up at the screen. 'I mean, look at his hair. It's just so . . . GOOD!'

'Ooh, he's the greatest mayor Shnozville has ever had!' cooed Bunny. 'I remember when he cut the ribbon at the opening of Bunny Deli. His hair couldn't have looked better!'

Jamjar did her little cough again. 'Actually that was Norman who cut the ribbon,' she said all seriously.

'Who's Norman?' I asked, and Not Bird shouted 'NOT!' again.

'Norman is Mayor Goodhair's pet pair of hover-scissors!' said Twoface. 'You really should know this stuff if you want to be a real superhero like me, Future Ratbums!'

Jamjar ignored Twoface and turned to me. 'It's a well-known fact that hover-scissors can't hold themselves back if there's something that needs snipping!' she said.

'Fascinating,' yawned Twoface, and Not Bird sniggled.

Not that I had time for that to annoy me, because the Shnozville Town Square clock had just struck seven billion.

SEVEN BILLION O'CLOCK ON THE DOT

A shiny black UFO appeared from behind a bright green cloud and a hatch in its bum slid open. A rainbow-coloured beam shot out of the hole and Mayor Goodhair floated down the middle of it.

'Good mornkeels, fellow Shnozvillians!' he boomed, landing on a little stage next to the draped-over statue. 'How does my hair look today?'

'GOOD!' cried the crowd.

Mayor Goodhair was wearing bright white trainers and a sparkly blue suit. Perched on top of his perfect hair sat a red cap with 'MAYOR' written on it. Next to him floated his pet pair of hover-scissors, Norman.

'How nice of you to turn out like this for my nine hundred and seventy-twelfth birthday!' he smiled. 'I hope you're enjoying the free food and drink?'

'That's a point,' I whispered to Jamjar. 'Where's the grub?'

Jamjar twizzled her eyes up at the sky. Loads of tiny different-coloured clouds that I hadn't noticed before were floating around like pillows.

'What in the name of unkeelness are THOSE?' I said.

'Call one over and find out!' smiled Jamjar.

I scratched my bum, feeling a bit stupid about the idea of talking to a cloud. 'Erm . . . here, Cloudy!' I said, and a little pink cloud drifted over and floated just above my head. 'Now what?'

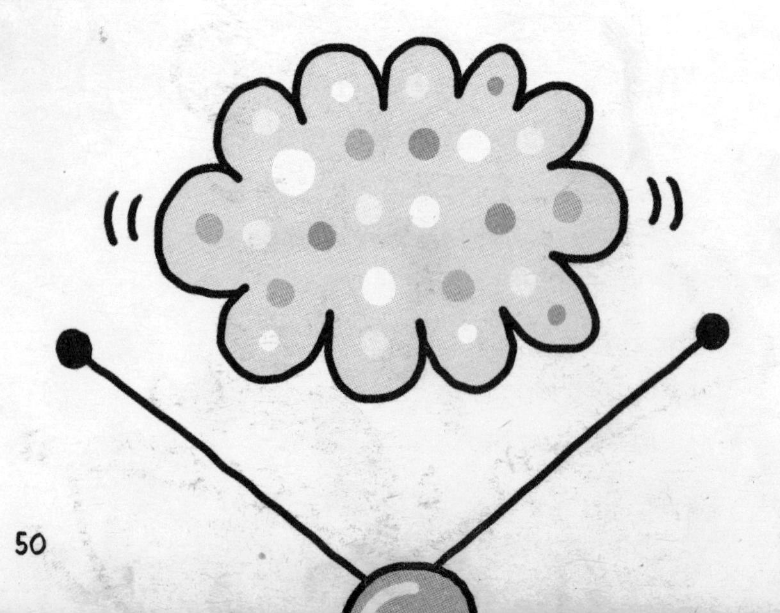

'NOT!' chirped Not Bird, and Twoface chuckled.

'Open your mouth!' said Jamjar, so I opened my mouth and the cloud started to rain.

'Pink Lemonade - my favourite!' I gurgled, as fizzy pink raindrops pitter-pattered down my throat.

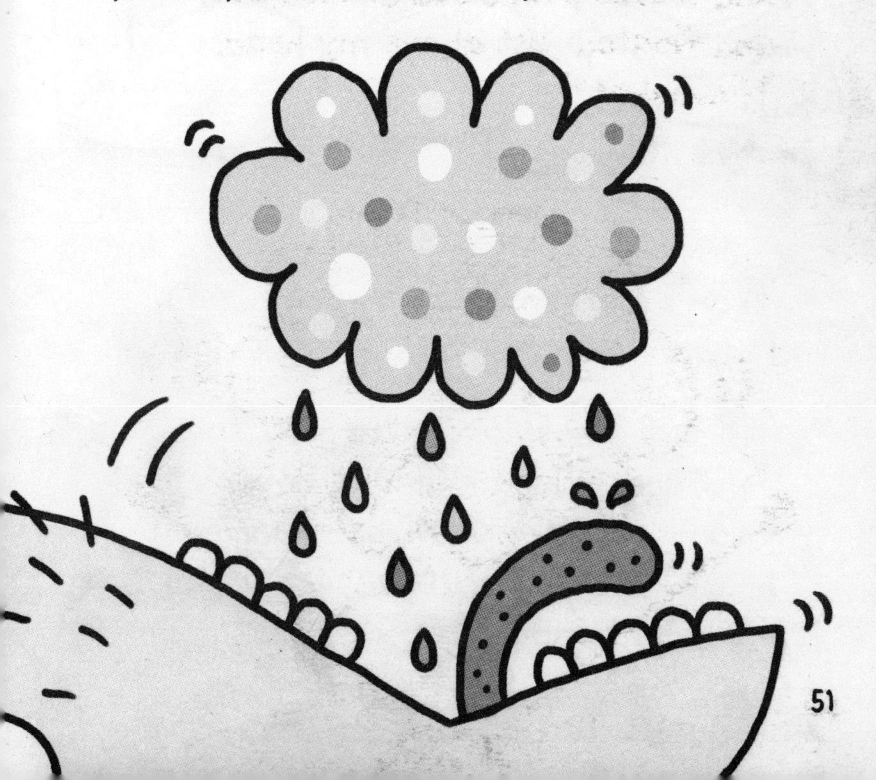

'How about a snack?' said Splorg, and he whistled. 'Here boy!' he called, and I spotted a hot dog galloping towards me. It stopped at my feet and barked.

'I can't eat him, he's way too cute!' I said.

'It's just a hot dog, Ratfingers!' said Twoface, picking it up and slotting it into his mouth. 'Mmm, good doggy!' he smiled, and a muffled woof echoed inside his tummy.

I ignored Twoface and did a whistle. Another hot dog ran over and I lifted it up to my mouth and bit it in half. It really was delicious, even though I felt a bit guilty.

'And now for my favourite part!' boomed Mayor Goodhair, pointing at the giant presents. 'The Grand Unwrapping!'

'Who buys all these statues for him?' I spluttered.

'Nobody,' said Bunny. 'Mayor Goodhair's so rich he buys his own presents!'

Mayor Goodhair clicked his fingers and Norman, his pet pair of hover-scissors, floated up to the bright red ribbon that was tied around the yellow sheet covering the statue.

'Ooh a ribbon,' squeaked Norman, swishing his blades open. 'I just can't resist!'

He swished his blades shut, snipping the ribbon in half, and the sheet flopped to the floor revealing a concrete Mayor Goodhair standing on top of a pillar.

'Another statue of me - just what I've always wanted!' beamed the mayor, and the crowd cheered.

Norman flew down towards one of the mayor's trouser pockets and slid himself into it. 'Hover-scissors get extremely tired after snipping a ribbon,' explained Jamjar. 'He'll need a nice nap now.'

'O-K . . .' I said, thinking how ridikeelous the future could be sometimes.

Mayor Goodhair turned to the floating pink parcel. 'And who bought me this great big one?' he asked.

'I thought you said he bought his own pressies?' I whispered to Bunny.

'Must be from a secret admirer!' she giggled.

A humungazoid label was hanging off the pink parcel. 'Somebody flip that tag round so I can read it, would you?' smiled Mayor Goodhair.

Not Bird flew up to the label and turned it over with his beak. 'Happy bday!' said the mayor, reading out what was written on it. Underneath the writing was a big black 'X' for a kiss.

'Ahh, that's nice!' smiled Splorg, as the mayor began to frown.

'Hmmm, there's something about that handwriting that rings a bell . . .' he mumbled, as the ground shook beneath me and the crowd started to scream.

THE UNINVITED GUEST

I turned round to see a giant metal scorpion appear from between two skyscrapers. I peered into the cockpit and gasped.

'It's Mr X!'

Mr X grimaced down at the crowd, his teeth jaggedy like a dinosaur's. 'How nice of you all to turn out like this for Mayor Goodhair's birthday!' he boomed.

Bill Aardvark narrowed his eyes on the hover-screen above our heads. 'Something tells me Mr X didn't really mean that,' he said, and Cecelia rolled her eyes.

Mayor Goodhair peered up at the label hanging off the floating pink parcel and snapped his fingers. 'That "X" isn't a kiss, it's Mr X's signature!' he cried.

'Got it in one, Mr Mayor!' cackled Mr X. 'Happy birthday, old pal!'

Jamjar pulled her Triangulator out of her pocket. She pointed it at the ginormous floating parcel and pressed a button.

JAMJAR'S TRIANGULATOR

'According to my Triangulator, the parameters of that cuboid's diametrics are disproportionate to its bio-quadrant.'

'Ooh, you are a clever clogs!' said Bunny, giving Jamjar a cuddle. 'Now, what did that all mean?'

'I don't think that birthday present is going to be a very nice surprise,' muttered Jamjar as it thudded to the ground, making the whole square shake.

NORMAN WAKES UP

'Happy-birth-keels-to-Mayor-Good-hair!' sang Mr X as Norman peeked out of the mayor's trouser pocket.

He swivelled his sleepy eyes up at the yellow ribbon that was wrapped around the parcel and started to fly through the air towards it. 'Ooh a ribbon, my favourite!' he squeaked.

'No Norman, don't do it – it's a trap!' cried Jamjar as Norman swished his blades open and snipped the ribbon in half. It fluttered to the ground and the wrapping paper started to fall away.

'Gulp, the whole thing's unwrapping itself!' said Splorg, turning round and speed-walking back the way we'd come.

I looked up at the giant pink pressie. A humungazoid muddy hand was reaching out from inside the wrapping paper.

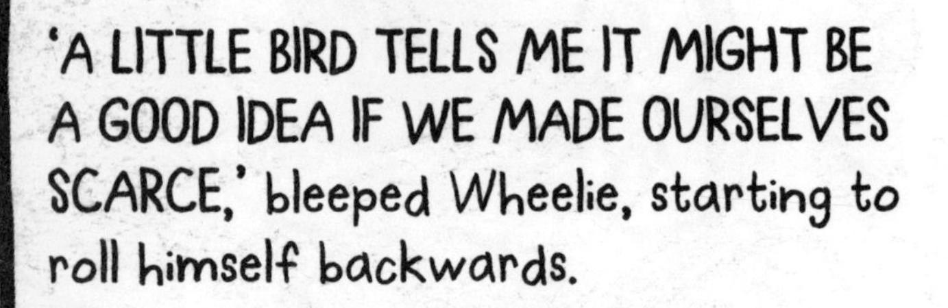

'A LITTLE BIRD TELLS ME IT MIGHT BE A GOOD IDEA IF WE MADE OURSELVES SCARCE,' bleeped Wheelie, starting to roll himself backwards.

screeched Not Bird, turning round in mid-air.

'This way!' cried Jamjar, leading us towards a passageway between two buildings. A hot dog was following us, and I bent down and picked it up, popping it into my mouth.

Which was the last thing I did before the whole day went completely wrong.

GOZO THE VENDING MACHINE MONSTER

The sound of an enormous foot stomping on the ground echoed around the square.

'CAN'T . . . EVEN . . . LOOK . . .' trembled Splorg, as Bunny twizzled her head round and stared up.

You know when you're watching an old black-and-white horror movie on TV and the monster appears and everyone's face turns white, and their eyes open wide and they scream? That's what Bunny was doing right now.

'M-M-M-M-MONSTER!!!' she wailed, waggling all ten of her arms in the air.

I swivelled on the spot and tilted my head upwards. There, next to Mayor Goodhair's brand spanking new statue, stood the most ginormousest, made-out-of-muddest, three-eyed-est monster I'd ever seen.

The monster blinked his three eyes and peered down at the square. He towered over the sock tree he was standing next to and on his tummy was a big plastic see-through window.

Behind the window, inside the monster's stomach, were a few rows of shelves. Next to them, sticking out from his muddy skin, was a line of buttons and a slot for giant coins to go into. Underneath the window was a big hatch.

'Say hello, Gozo!' boomed Mr X.

'HELLOOO GOZO!' roared Gozo, stomping his foot on a manhole cover with a picture of Mayor Goodhair's face carved into it.

'Hey, watch my new manhole cover,' cried the mayor. 'I only just replaced them all last month!'

I Future-Ratboy-zoomed my eyes in on Gozo and frowned. 'Erm, does that gigantic monster's tummy looks at all familikeels to any of you lot?' I whispered, as quietly as possible so it wouldn't hear me.

'NOT!' screeched Not Bird, and Twoface shook his head.

'Never seen anything like it in my life,' he said.

Jamjar slipped the Triangulator out of her pocket and pointed it in the direction of Gozo's belly-window. 'Interestikeels . . .' she muttered. 'These readings indicate a four billion percent possibility of a favourable subjunctive!'

'What's that mean, in normal speak?' said Splorg.

'Seems Mr X has been busy converting our pal The Wise Old Vending Machine into, well . . . THAT!'

'Ah-ha, I knew his tummy looked familikeels!' said Twoface, and Not Bird nodded.

'You monster!' I cried, and I wasn't talking to Gozo. I'd turned to face Mr X, who was still inside his giant metal scorpion, grinning like an evil baddy. 'What have you done with The Wise Old Vending Machine?!'

GOZO EATS ALL THE BOOKS

'Oh, I just made a few alterations!' smiled Mr X, opening the hatch on his scorpion, jumping out and landing in Gozo's palm. 'Show 'em what you can do, Gozo!'

Mr X winked at Gozo, and the gigantic muddy beast swivelled its head, looking around. 'MMM, BUILDING!' it boomed, stomping over to Shnozville Library, which was sitting in the corner of the square minding its own business.

'Hey, keep that thing away from my lovely library!' cried Jamjar as Gozo grabbed the building by its roof and tore the whole thing out of the ground in one go.

'Relax Jamjar,' said Twoface. 'Ever heard of an eBook? This is the future, you know!'

Gozo lifted the library up to his wide-open mouth and slotted it in like a giant cake. 'YUM YUM!' he smiled, rubbing his window belly.

'And now for the fun part!' cackled Mr X, pointing at the shelves behind the see-through plastic.

THE FUN PART

A cardboard box was slowly being lowered on to the bottom shelf by a robotic arm. The box had a photo of Shnozville Library on the front of it, with the words 'SHNOZVILLE LIBRARY' written at the top.

'Waaahhh! The library's INSIDE the vending machine!' screamed Jamjar.

'It looks like a toy dolls' house, Bill!' chuckled Cecelia Twizzlefrump.

Splorg scratched his head. 'How in the keelness did that happen?' he said.

Mr X sniggered to himself and jumped out of the monster's hand, on to the little stage. 'Oh, Gozo here's got quite a few tricks up his sleeve. Isn't that right, Gozo?' he asked.

The giant muddy monster belched.

BURP!

'Poowee, that burp stinks of library!' cried someone from the crowd.

'Wise Old Vending Machine!' I cried, trying to see if our pal The Wise Old Vending Machine was still inside Gozo somewhere.

'NOT!' screeched Not Bird.

'It's no good, Ratboy,' sighed Jamjar, pointing her Triangulator at the muddy monster. 'Mr X has eradicated his core fundamentals . . .'

'EH?' bleeped Wheelie.

'Whatever's left of The Wise Old Vending Machine inside that horrible beast has been completely evilised!' said Jamjar.

Gozo licked his lips. 'SUMFIN HEALFY NOW!' he roared, stomping over to the sock tree he'd first appeared behind.

'Oh no, not a sock tree!' cried Splorg, as Gozo yanked it out of the ground and chomped it down in one.

The sock tree appeared inside the monster's belly, shrink-wrapped like a sprig of broccoli down the supermarket. A sticker on the plastic said 'SOCK TREE' on it in multicoloured letters.

After that, Gozo ate a hover-postbox, then a bench that an old granny with a really warty nose had been sitting on until three seconds before, then a lamppost.

'Anything else you fancy, Gozo?' said Mr X.

The monster patted his tummy and looked down at the brand new concrete statue of Mayor Goodhair. 'CONCRETEY!' he grinned.

'NOT MY BRAND NEW STATUE!'

cried Mayor Goodhair, as Gozo's brown muddy hand reached down and grabbed the statue. 'B-but I only unveiled that one just now!'

Gozo blinked his three eyes and popped the statue into his mouth.

'W-what is this madness?' stuttered the mayor, as the statue was lowered on to a shelf next to the lamppost, packaged up like some kind of giant concrete action figure.

MAYOR GOODHAIR
STATUE

Mr X smiled to himself. 'Think of old Gozo here as a sort of gigantic vending machine,' he said, peering proudly through the window at all the stuff inside.

Mayor Goodhair looked up at the coin slot on Gozo's chest. 'You want money?' he shouted, pulling a fat leather wallet out of his pocket. 'I could buy my statue back from you!'

'Please! Put your wallet away, Mayor Goodhair!' sneered Mr X. 'Your measly coins aren't nearly big enough for Gozo's slot!'

Gozo rubbed his plastic see-through belly and it rumbled. 'ME STILL HUNGRY!' he roared, looking around for what he was going to eat next.

YOU WON'T LIKE GOZO WHEN HE'S HUNGRY

'Uh-oh!' sniggered Mr X. 'I probably shouldn't have programmed Gozo to get so grumpy when he's peckish,' he said. 'But . . . I did!'

'WHAT ELSE ME WANT TO EAT?' grumbled the monster.

The trouble was he'd chomped pretty much one of everything there was to offer in Shnozville Town Square. Apart from a real live person.

'MMM, NICE CROWD!'

said Gozo, peering down at us all.

'Run!' cried an old man with seven ears, starting to run around in circles, which was probably the worst thing you could do if you were trying to stop a giant person-eating monster from noticing you.

Gozo opened his hand like a claw and hovered it over the crowd as if it was one of those metal grabber games you get at the arcade.

'Don't worry, I'll save you, children!' cried Bunny, waggling her ten arms in the air. 'Cooee! Eat me, Mr Bozo!'

'No, Bunny!' I shouted, forward-rolling towards her. I grabbed all ten of her arms - five in each hand - and slotted them into ten of her pockets, then rolled her on to the floor and sat on top of her.

Which took about as long to do as you'd think. Which meant Gozo had had plenty of time to spot us.

boomed Gozo, reaching down to grab us both.

'Why don't you go and eat someone your own size!' I shouted, as Twoface jumped on top of me.

'Think you're the superhero do you, Ratboy?' he cried, his bum landing right in my face. 'Well two can play at that game!'

'Stop it you two, you're squashing Bunny!' yelped Splorg, pulling at Twoface's arm.

'Run, Splorg - save yourself!' I cried, as Gozo's fingernail scraped the tip of my TV aerial.

'NOT!' screeched Not Bird.

'SHUT UP NOT BIRD!' I cried.

'Stop bickering, you two!' warbled Bunny from underneath us all.

'IS THERE ANYTHING I CAN DO TO HELP, SIRS AND MADAM?' bleeped Wheelie, rolling over.

Jamjar skidded to a stop next to my head and pointed her Triangulator at Gozo's claw. 'I'll try and reverse the digital polarity – it might buy us a few billiseconds!' she shouted.

But it was too late.

'NOT!' screeched Not Bird again, as the shadow of Gozo's hand made everything go dark and I got ready to be eaten alive by a giant vending machine monster.

You know when it's all dark and you're being eaten alive by a giant vending machine monster and you feel his teeth biting through your tummy, slicing you in half like a hot dog?

That wasn't happening to me right now.

Everything went quiet and the lights came back on.

'Wh-what happened?' I stuttered, looking around. I was lying on the ground next to Bunny.

'I'm alive!' cried Splorg, dusting himself down and looking around. Jamjar was staring up into the sky, her mouth hanging wide open.

'Where's Twoface? And Not Bird!?' I asked.

'You don't even want to know!' chuckled Bill Aardvark from the hover-screen, and I twizzled round to look where he was looking.

There, about three sock trees' height above me, inside Gozo's plastic see-through belly, shrink-wrapped in a plastic and cardboard packet, sat Twoface and Not Bird.

'OH. MY. UNKEELNESS,' I said.

'Twoface!' cried Splorg.

'Not Bird!' warbled Bunny.

'Hee hee!' cackled Mr X.

'I have to say, I'm really enjoying this little show!' he said. 'It almost makes me wish I CARED about somebody other than myself!'

'Ooh, you horrible little man!' cried Bunny, and Mr X stopped laughing.

At first I thought the reason Mr X had stopped laughing was because Bunny had called him horrible.

Then I realised it was something else.

Gozo had turned round and tilted his eyebrows even further into their REALLY angry positions. Not only that, he was walking towards Mr X.

'Uh-oh, looks like he's hungry again,' said Splorg.

'Watch out!' cried Jamjar, diving out of the way as Gozo stepped over the top of us.

'There there, Gozo,' said Mr X, scrabbling backwards. 'You don't want to eat me! I haven't showered for . . . ever!'

Gozo grabbed Mr X by the scruff of the neck and dangled him under his nostrils, giving him a sniff to see if he was worth chomping.

The great muddy beast breathed in through his nose. Then scrunched his eyes shut.

'POO-WEE!' he roared, flinging his master into the nearest sock tree.

'OUCH! OOF! ARGH! EEK!'

cried Mr X, falling through the tree, bonking his head on every branch along the way.

The crowd that'd gathered for Mayor Goodhair's birthday had run off in every direction, and Mr X's screams echoed round the empty square.

'Ooh, that has GOT to hurt!' chuckled Cecelia Twizzlefrump as Shnozville News's hover-cameras zoomed in on Mr X, lying dazed on the floor.

'What happened?' grinned Mr X.

Grinning seemed like a weird thing to do after falling through a sock tree.

He sat up and looked around. 'Hey, where's Gozo off to?' he said, pointing over our shoulders and we all twizzled our heads. Gozo was stomping out of Shnozville Town Square, off to find something new to eat.

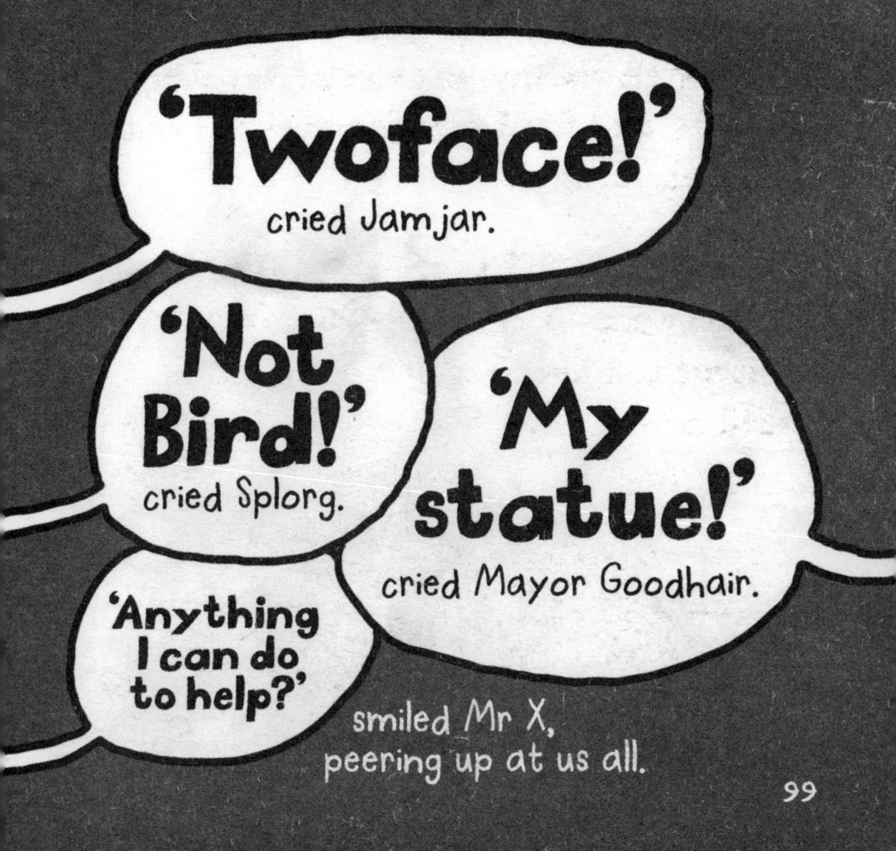

I Future-Ratboy-zoomed my eyes in on Mr X and did a superhero frown. 'Hmmm, there's something fishy going on here,' I said.

'Mmm, fish!' said Mr X. 'I love fish! Not to eat of course. I just like cuddling them!'

Bunny scratched her nose. 'What's got into him?' she said, looking down at Mr X.

Mr X smiled up at Bunny. 'Hello, Mrs Bunny old friend!' he said. 'I see you have an itch there. May I scratch it for you?'

'No thank you very much,' said Bunny, staring at him like he'd gone mad.

I sat down on the edge of the hover-pavement, my feet in the gutter. Next to me was one of Mayor Goodhair's new manhole covers. Not that that had anything to do with what was happening right now.

'We have to get Twoface and Not Bird back!' I said. And I waited to hear Not Bird shout 'NOT!'

But there was just silence.

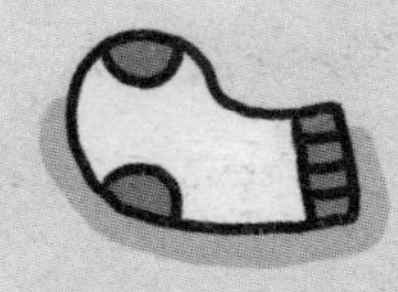

THE HOVER-RUBBISH TRUCK

'Ratboy, watch your feet!' cried Splorg, and I heard a hoovering sort of noise start up a little further down the hover-pavement.

'Here comes a hover-rubbish truck,' said Mayor Goodhair. On the side of the truck was the number 27. 'That'll clear this mess up, at least,' he sighed.

I looked around the square. The mayor wasn't joking. The place looked like a giant vending machine monster had hit it.

Mayor Goodhair took his cap off and walked up to Mr X, bending over to peer into his eyes. 'Now look here, Mr X,' he said. 'I demand you return my statue immediately!'

Mr X grinned. 'Mayor Goodhair, old pal!' he said, holding out his hand to shake the mayor's. 'Fantastic hair as always!'

'Never mind my stupid hair!' cried the mayor. 'Show me where the OFF switch is on that monster of yours!'

Mr X thought for a billisecond. 'Hmm, can't remember!' he grinned.

'Can't remember?!' wailed the mayor.

Bill Aardvark chuckled, his six rows of bright white teeth glistening. 'Looks like those bonks on the head wiped Mr X's memory!' he said.

'You don't say, Bill,' said Cecelia Twizzlefrump. 'Not only that, they seem to have turned him into a goody-goody as well!'

'Well this won't do at all!' growled Mayor Goodhair, stomping off in the direction Gozo had gone. 'You lot keep your eyes on Mr X while I go and get that monster back!' he shouted over his shoulder.

Bunny watched the mayor go round the corner, followed by his hover-scissors. She shook her head and turned to us.

'We're not safe out here with that Bozo thing chomping everything in sight,' she said. 'I think we'd better head back to Bunny Deli and work out what to do next, don't you?'

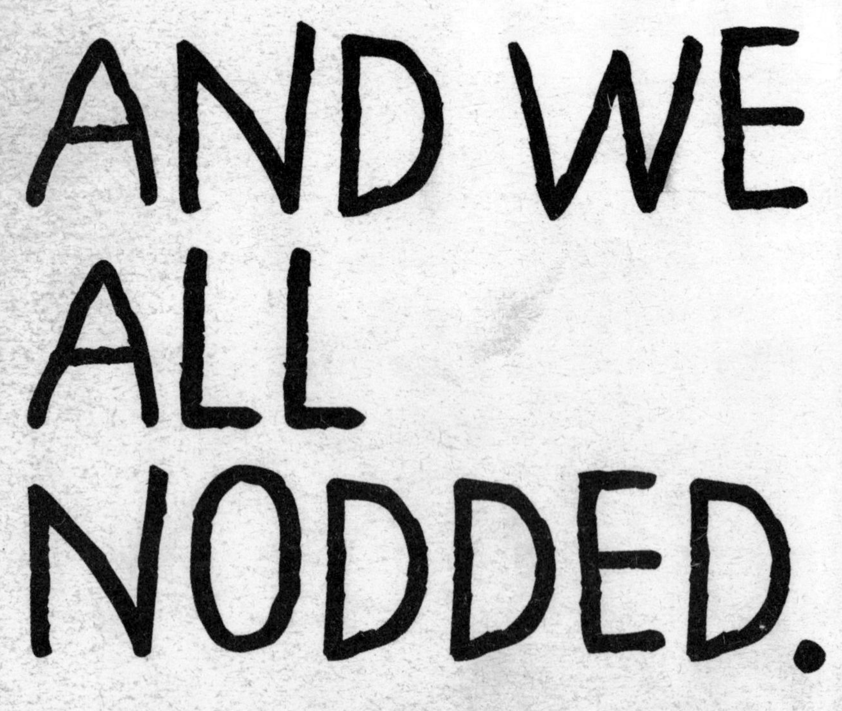

BACK AT BUNNY DELI

'Mmm, delish!' smiled Mr X, tucking into his Cheesebleurgher Meal Deal back at Bunny Deli. He'd followed me, Jamjar, Splorg, Wheelie and Bunny there from Shnozville Town Square, being weirdly nice the whole way.

'I still don't get why HE's here,' said Splorg, bits of Cheesebleurgher spluttering over the table towards Mr X.

'Mr X is the only one who knows how Gozo works,' explained Jamjar. 'I haven't puzzled out exactly what's going on with him yet, but as long as he behaves himself, he can stay.'

'So, how are we gonna get Twoface and Not Bird back?' I said, keeping one of my Future-Ratboy-eyes on Mr X. I took a bite of my Cheesebleurgher and a hover-screen fizzled to life above our heads.

'This just in . . .' crackled Cecelia Twizzlefrump's voice. I looked up and saw her ginormous fake smiles gleaming down at me from the screen. 'Some HILARIOUS footage of Mr X falling through that sock tree earlier today!'

'Ooh, that blooming Shnozville News,' grumbled Bunny. 'Twoface and Not Bird are inside the belly of a monster who's chomping his way through town and all they can do is play silly videos!'

The hover-screen cut to a video of Gozo throwing Mr X into the sock tree. 'OUCH! OOF! ARGH! EEK!' he cried again, bouncing off the branches and landing on the pavement.

'Oh come on, Bunny,' chuckled Mr X. 'You've got to admit it's pretty funny!'

I Future-Ratboy-zoomed my eyes in on Mr X – not the real-life one sitting opposite me at the table, but the one on the screen – and noticed something weird. 'What was that?' I said.

'What was what?' asked Splorg, slurping on his cup of cola-flavoured puddle.

'I'm not sure,' I said. 'It looked like something fell out of Mr X's costume . . .'

Jamjar glanced up at the giant hover-screen. 'Hey, Cecelia!' she shouted. 'Can you replay that footage, but in slow motion?'

That's one of the keel things about living in the future – you can talk to the people on TV.

The screen went fuzzy as the footage rewound. 'OK, now play in slow-mo!' said Cecelia Twizzlefrump, and we all watched the clip again, but ten times slower.

'Zoom in on Mr X!' I shouted, as he fell out of the tree and landed bum-first on the hover-pavement. 'There!' I said. 'See that thing falling out of his hood?'

Bill Aardvark pressed a button and the screen froze. Sure enough, a tiny little spiky-looking clump of something had landed on the pavement next to Mr X.

'WHAT IN THE NAME OF UNKEELNESS IS THAT?' bleeped Wheelie, waggling his arm at the screen.

IT'S A THINGY!

Bunny clicked two of her millions of fingers. 'It's a THINGY!' she said.

'What's a THINGY?' asked Splorg.

Jamjar pulled her Triangulator out and started tapping its screen. 'Says here that THINGYS were a popular cereal from way back,' she said. 'Apparently they stopped making them after getting complaints they were too spiky.'

'Ooh, they WERE spiky!' cooed Bunny. 'But they softened up nicely once you'd put the milk on them. Funny tasting things . . .'

Mr X stared up at the hover-screen. 'Not that I ever got the chance to find out!' he smiled, sadly.

Splorg scratched his bald blue head. 'I don't see what any of this has got to do with us getting Twoface and Not Bird back,' he said.

But I just ignored him. There was something about that THINGY thingy that was making my ratty super senses tingle.

'How come you never tried a THINGY, Mr X?' I asked.

'It's a long story!' beamed Mr X, and our noses all drooped, because everybody knows that long stories are . . .

BORING!

THE LONG STORY

'And that's the end of my long story!' smiled Mr X about half an hour later. I don't know why he was smiling, because it was the saddest story I've ever heard.

'I CANNOT BELIEVE MR X AND MAYOR GOODHAIR WERE IN AN ORPHANAGE TOGETHER WHEN THEY WERE KIDS,' bleeped Wheelie. 'OR THAT MAYOR GOODHAIR STOLE MR X'S BOWL OF THINGYS EVERY MORNING AND ATE THEM ALL HIMSELF!'

'I can't believe Mr X took half an hour to tell that story when you just summed it up in two sentences,' said Jamjar. 'We could've been rescuing Twoface and Not Bird in that time!'

Splorg nodded. 'We've GOT to get them out of that Gozo's belly and turn him off before he eats the whole of Shnozville.'

'Don't you remember though?' I said. 'Mr X has forgotten where the OFF switch is!'

Mr X tapped his hooded head. 'It's true,' he smiled. 'The old noggin's not been the same since Gozo chucked me into that sock tree.'

Jamjar, who'd been sitting quietly tapping on her Triangulator, looked up. 'There's still one thing I don't quite get,' she said. 'How did Mr X end up with a THINGY inside his costume?'

'That's a point,' I said, turning to Mr X. 'Any ideas?'

'Search me!' he grinned, pulling his hood off, and we all screamed.

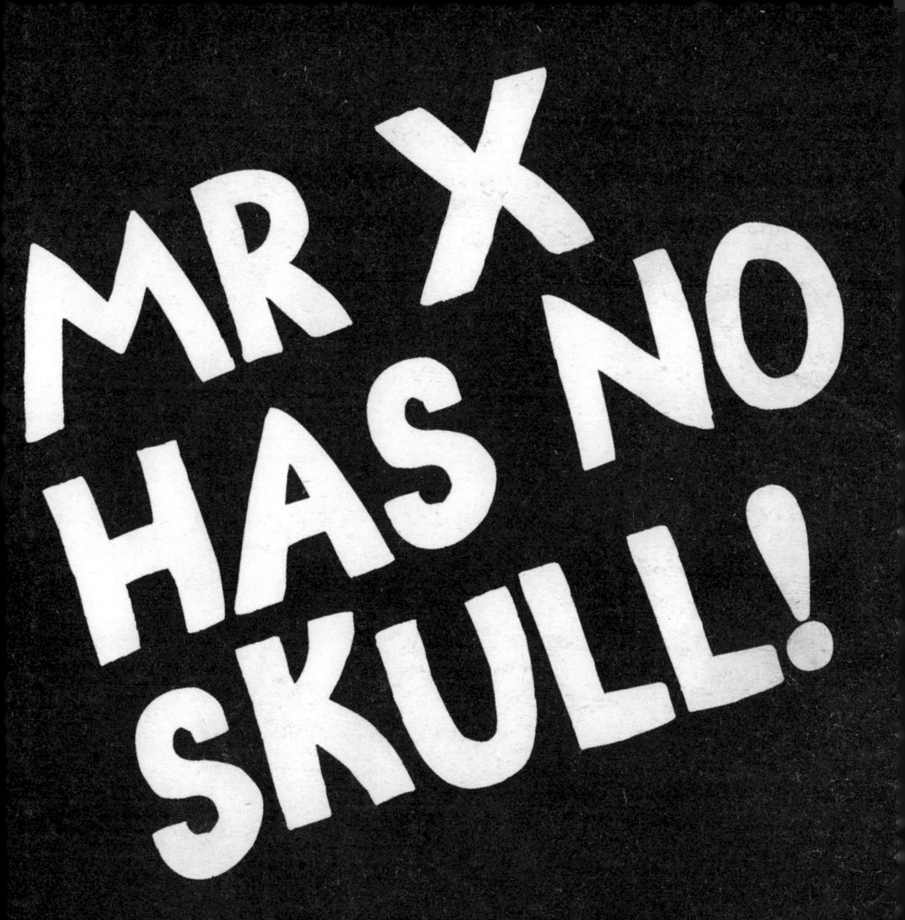

'Waaahhh! Naked brain!' cried Splorg, scraping backwards in his chair.

He was waggling his hand in the direction of Mr X's head – the top half of which looked like it'd been sliced off, revealing a glistening pink brain inside.

Mr X patted it and the whole thing jiggled like a jelly. 'What, this old thing?' he chuckled. 'It's always been like that! Why do you think I wear a hood?'

Jamjar peered into Mr X's open skull. And then she asked the most ridikeelous question I've ever heard.

'Mr X, can you remember any incidences in which a THINGY might've got lodged inside your head?' she said.

Mr X scratched his brain.
'Don't think so,' he said.

Jamjar's nose drooped.

'Apart from that one time when Mayor Goodhair was shooting THINGYS at my head through a straw for a whole week . . .' added Mr X.

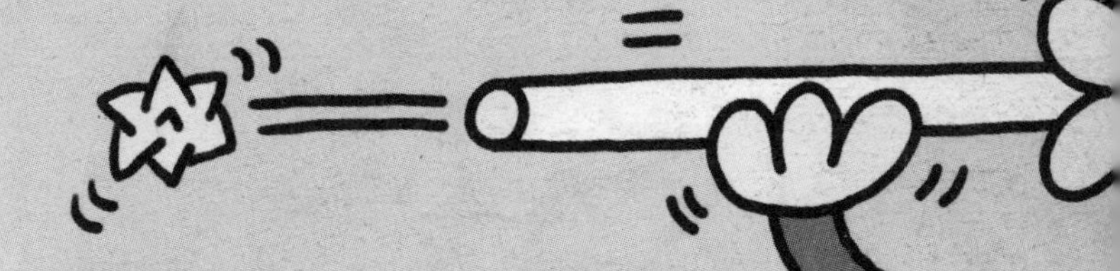

'That's it!' cried Jamjar, jumping out of her seat.

'WHAT'S WHAT, MA'AM?' bleeped Wheelie.

'Don't you see?' said Jamjar. 'It wasn't the bonks on his head that turned Mr X into a goody-goody – it was the THINGY falling out of his brain!'

'Are you saying,' I asked, 'that there's been a THINGY wedged in Mr X's brain all these years?'

'Exactly!' grinned Jamjar. 'And that's what's been making him so grumpy!'

Bunny crossed all ten of her arms. 'This is all very interestikeels,' she said, 'but I don't see how it gets us any closer to rescuing Twoface and Not Bird.'

'Ah ha, that's the thing!' said Jamjar. 'Now we know how to turn Mr X back into a baddy. All we have to do is get that THINGY back into his brain!'

'And why in the unkeelness would we want to do that?' squeaked Splorg.

'Because only the old, evil Mr X knows where Gozo's OFF switch is hidden!' cried Jamjar.

'Back to Shnozville Town Square to find that THINGY!'

shouted Jamjar, running out of Bunny Deli. 'Bunny, you stay here - and make sure you have a straw ready!'

'A straw?' said Bunny, scratching her chin. 'What in the keelness for?'

'To shoot the THINGY back into Mr X's brain of course!' said Jamjar, zooming down the road followed by me, Wheelie, Splorg and Mr X.

We skidded to a stop in Shnozville Town Square and I spotted the hover-rubbish truck from earlier, disappearing off round a corner.

The whole square sparkled as if a giant vending machine monster had never even been there.

'Where IS that THINGY?' I said, forward-rolling over to the sock tree Gozo had thrown Mr X into, and I looked around on the pavement underneath. But I couldn't see it anywhere.

Jamjar knocked on her head like it was a front door. 'Great bowls of cereal!' she said. 'It must've been hoovered up . . .'

'Follow that hover-rubbish truck!' cried Splorg, pointing to the corner where the truck had turned off.

'Hee hee, this is fun!' giggled Mr X, his brains wobbling as he ran.

'OOH, I LIKE THE LOOK OF THIS PLACE!'

bleeped Wheelie when we arrived at the entrance to Shnozville Town Dump. We'd followed the hover-rubbish truck the whole way there.

I walked through the big metal gates and glanced up at the mountain of rubbish piled up in front of us. There were scratched-up washing machines and crumpled cardboard boxes and loads of other thrown-away things, but mostly the mountain was made up of leaf socks.

Stacked up in front of the gates was a line of old manhole covers – the ones that'd been replaced last month. 'HELP YOURSELF!' said a sign rested up against them.

'Who'd want to help themselves to a boring old manhole cover?' I mumbled, noticing a queue of hover-rubbish trucks snaking up to the stinking heap, taking it in turns to dump their contents on top.

'Argh, which one is ours?' cried Splorg. I thought back to the hover-rubbish truck I'd seen in Shnozville Town Square. 'It's the one with 27 written on the side!' I said.

Wheelie patted me on the head with one of his coily arms. 'GOOD WORK, MASTER RATBOY, SIR,' he said. 'THERE IT IS.'

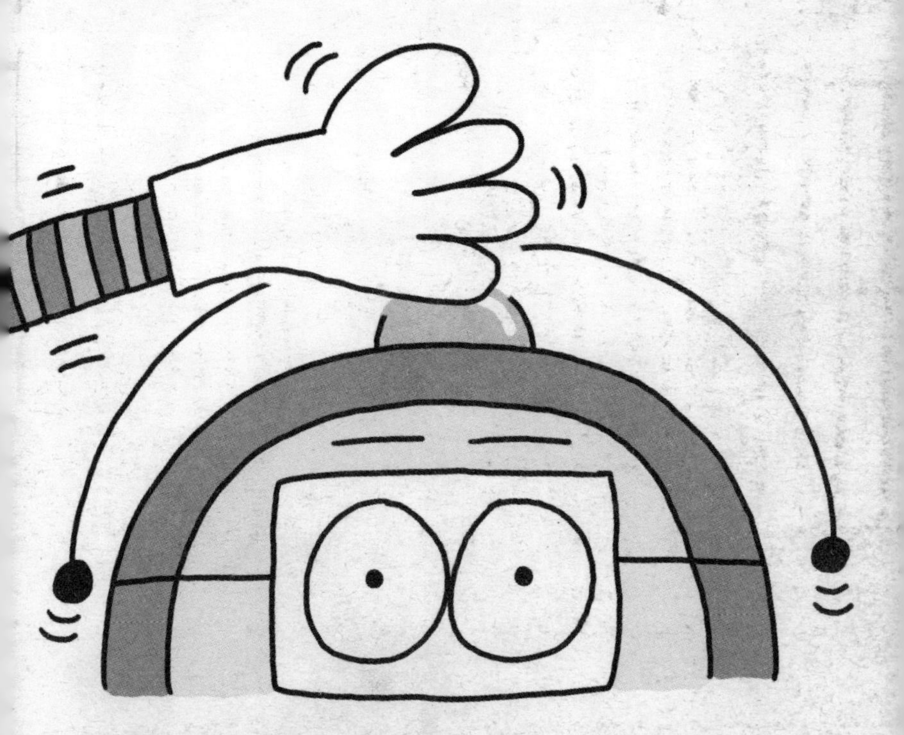

And I looked up and spotted our truck – the one with the THINGY inside it – at the front of the queue.

THE GREAT RUBBISH CHUTE

'Quick, before it tips all its rubbish on to the . . .' I cried, but it was too late. Hover-rubbish truck number 27 had tilted itself backwards, and everything inside was now on top of the mountain.

Just above the mountain hung a gigantic tube, a bit like a huge see-through straw, that disappeared off into the sky, as far as your eyes could see. 'What in the keelness is THAT?' I said, pointing up at it.

'That's The Great Rubbish Chute,' said Jamjar. 'It sucks rubbish out of the dump and spits it into space!'

'Eh?' I said. 'Doesn't that make a bit of a mess up in space?'

'Not at all,' smiled Jamjar. 'I'll explain it to you later. But right now we've got to hurry. The Great Rubbish Chute does a giant suck every ten minutes. If we're not quick, that THINGY will be gone forever!'

THE BIG HAIRY WOMAN

'I'm going in!' I shouted, forward-rolling towards the giant pile.

'Sorry mate, 'fraid I'm gonna 'ave to stop you there,' boomed a deep voice, and a giant hairy woman wearing a yellow helmet stepped out in front of me and held up her hand. 'No rummaging allowed.'

'DO YOU KNOW WHO YOU ARE TALKING TO, MA'AM?' bleeped Wheelie. 'THAT'S THE SHNOZVILLE SUPERHERO OF THE MONTH!'

The hairy woman glared down at me and licked her lips. I hadn't noticed until this point that she had a long curly tail and two pointy teeth like a cat's. 'Mmm, giant rat,' she purred. 'That's my favourite, that is . . .'

I Future-Rat-backed away, smiling nervously. 'OK, OK, I don't want any trouble,' I said, turning to face the gang. 'Looks like we're going to have to find another way . . .'

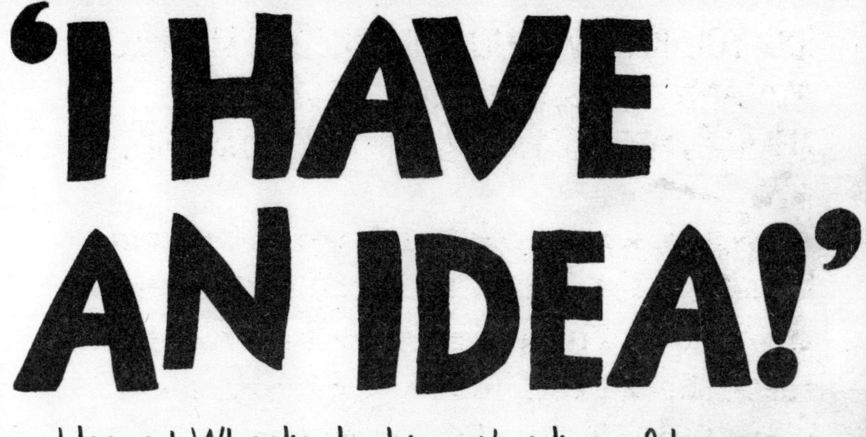

bleeped Wheelie, looking at a line of hover-bin bags queued up against the outside fence of Shnozville Town Dump. Every single one of them was filled to the top with leaf socks, just like outside Dr Smell's.

'What is it Wheelie?' asked Mr X.

Wheelie's lid flapped open and shut excitedly and we all held our noses to stop the stink going up them.

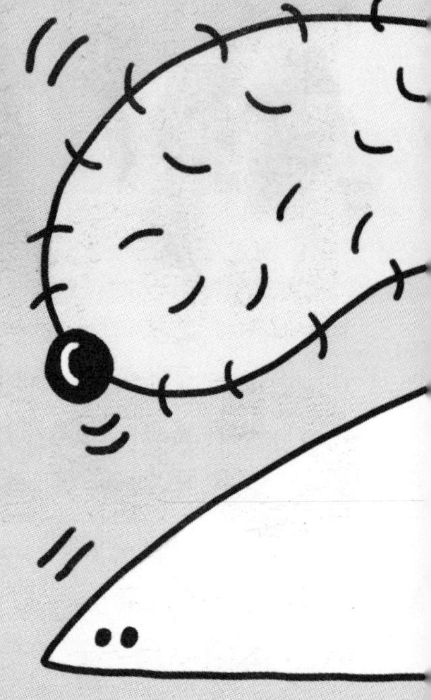

'I THOUGHT PERHAPS YOU COULD EACH HIDE YOURSELVES INSIDE ONE OF THOSE HOVER-BIN BAGS AND FLOAT UP TO THE RUBBISH MOUNTAIN DISGUISED AS LEAF SOCKS,' he bleeped. 'I'LL GO FIRST, SEEING AS I'M A REAL-LIFE BIN!'

We all looked at each other and smiled. 'That is the most ridikeelous plan I have ever heard,' said Jamjar. 'I love it!'

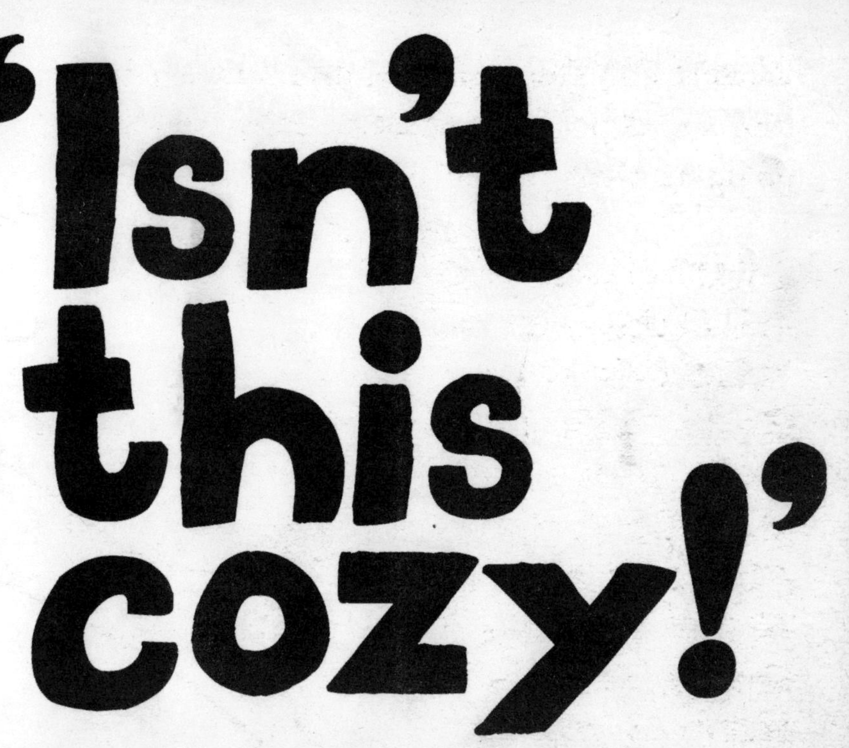

grinned Mr X as we squidged ourselves into a hover-bin bag each.

'OFF WE GO, GANG!' bleeped Wheelie, leading the way.

Splorg floated next to me, the tip of his great big blue nose sticking out of his hover-bin bag so he could breathe. 'Hey, I might get myself one of these!' he grinned. 'It's much easier than walking!'

The big hairy cat woman in the yellow helmet stepped out in front of Wheelie. 'Wot you got there, mate?' she grumbled.

'LEAF SOCKS,' bleeped Wheelie, acting all casual. 'JUST A FEW TRILLION OF THEM . . .'

The woman peered past Wheelie at me and the gang, hidden inside our hover-bin bags. 'Tell me about it,' she groaned, pointing at the mountain of leaf socks behind him. 'All right, this lot looks fine, through you go.'

Wheelie carried on towards the rubbish mountain, and I glanced over at Jamjar. 'Well that was easier than I thought!' I giggled.

We floated round to the back of the mountain and climbed out of the hover-bin bags. 'How are we EVER going to find that THINGY in this pile of old rubbish?' whispered Splorg.

And that was when I heard the whooshy sound.

'Waaahhh!!! The Great Rubbish Chute – it's started!' cried Jamjar, her hair getting sucked towards the giant straw.

Leaf socks and crumpled up cardboard boxes started flying into the tube. 'There's the THINGY!' cried Splorg. 'I just saw it zoom off up the chute!'

I looked up and spotted the spiky little thing hurtling towards space. 'There's only one thing for it – we're going to have to follow the THINGY!' shouted Jamjar, as my feet lifted off the floor.

Have you ever imagined what it's like to be a droplet of lemonade being sucked up a straw towards someone's mouth? Well that's how it felt zooming through The Great Rubbish Chute.

I plopped out the end of it and landed smack on my bum in another pile of rubbish. Except this one was ever so slightly bigger than the one in Shnozville Dump. This one was the size of a planet.

I looked up and spotted the Earth, spinning far away in the sky, the size of a tennis ball. A long winding tube - The Great Rubbish Chute - snaked all the way from the tennis ball to here.

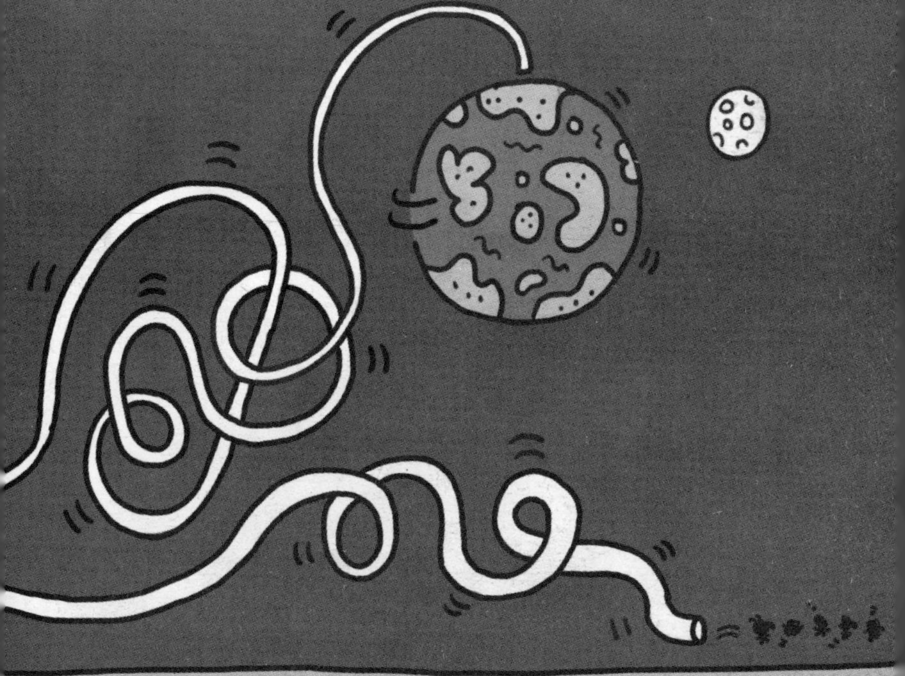

'Erm, where exactly are we?' I said.

'We're sitting on top of the biggest rubbish bin in the known universe!' said Jamjar.

'OOH, WHAT AN HONOUR,' bleeped Wheelie.

I looked at Jamjar, waiting for her to explain what was going on. 'Remember how I said that The Great Rubbish Chute sucks all the rubbish out of the dump and spits it into space?' she said.

I NODDED.

'Well this is where it spits it,' she said.

'But how come the rubbish isn't floating around everywhere?' I asked.

'Because we're on the Planet Bin!' she grinned.

I said.

'That's right!' said Jamjar. 'It comes with its own built-in gravity – that's why the rubbish isn't floating around everywhere.'

Wheelie flapped his lid open and shut. 'A WHOLE PLANET COMPLETELY DEDICATED TO BEING A BIN,' he bleeped. 'HOW GLORIOUS.'

The Great Rubbish Chute rattled above us and spat out another serving of junk.

'Argh, stupid leaf socks!' cried Splorg, lifting one off his head. 'How are we ever going to find that THINGY with all this rubbish everywhere?!'

I waggled my ratty nostrils, pretending I could smell as well as Dr Smell. 'Poo-wee, is that the stink of a quitter?' I said. 'Come on Splorg, I know you better than that!'

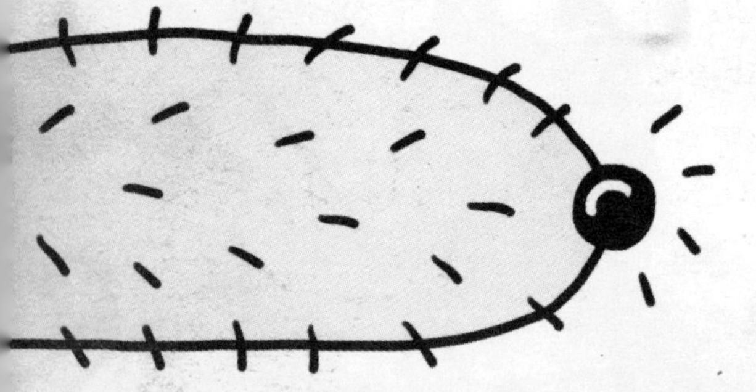

Jamjar chuckled at my Dr Smell impression. 'Ratboy's right, Splorg. Let's start looking,' she smiled.

And that's when I spotted Dr Smell dressed up as an old lady, walking towards us.

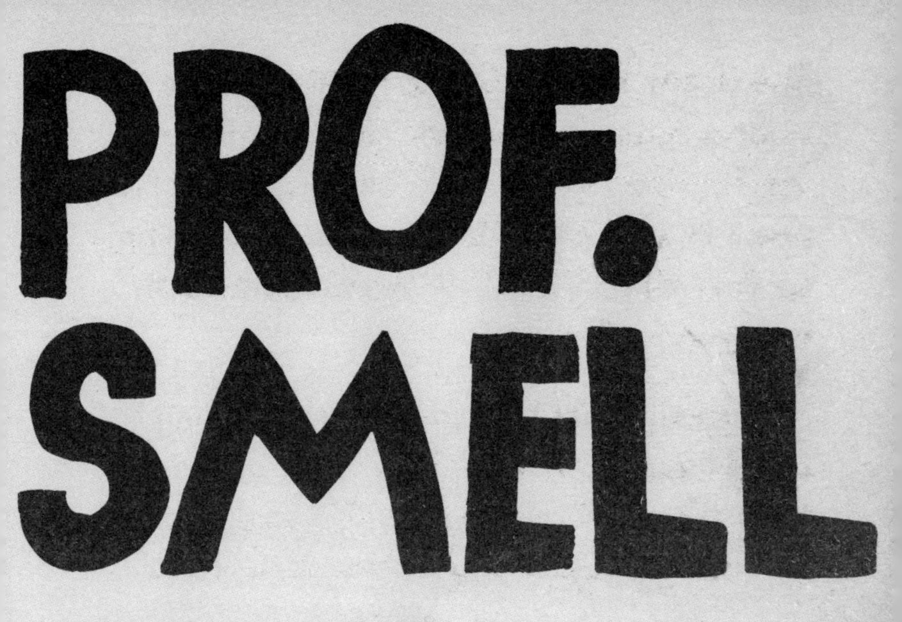

'Dr Smell!' grinned Mr X. 'What in the keelness are you doing here? That's a nice dress you're wearing!'

Dr Smell wrinkled up his nose. 'You must be mistaking me for my son, dear,' he said in a high voice.

We all looked at each other and sniggled. 'You're Dr Smell's mum?' asked Jamjar.

'Professor Smell at your service,' smiled the lady, shaking all our hands. 'Welcome to Planet Bin!'

'What's a beautiful young lady like you doing up here all on her own?' said Mr X, and I tried to work out how old Mr X must be, because Professor Smell didn't look very young to me.

'I've been living up here for years,' warbled Professor Smell. 'I came to do some research and never left – there's just so much to sniff.'

Splorg glanced around. 'But you're living in a BIN,' he cried.

'I know, isn't it fantastic!' said Professor Smell. 'Apart from the Space Hedgehogs, of course.'

"SPACE HEDGE-HOGS?"

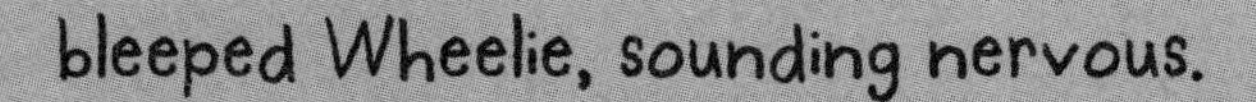

bleeped Wheelie, sounding nervous.

Professor Smell's nostrils tilted into their serious positions. 'Yes, nasty little critters,' she whispered, looking around. 'I say little – they're the size of hover-cars!'

'I DO NOT LIKE THE SOUND OF THOSE THINGS ONE TINY BIT,' bleeped Wheelie, and Mr X put an arm round his plastic belly.

'Don't worry Wheelie,' he smiled, giving him a cuddle. 'I'll protect you.'

Jamjar, who'd been quietly staring at Professor Smell's wrinkly old nose, glanced over at Mr X's glistening brain like she was coming up with one of her plans.

'What are you thinking, Jamjar?' I asked, and she clicked her fingers.

'I think I might've come up with a brilliant and smelly plan,' she smiled.

'What in name of nostrils are you talking about, young lady?'

said Professor Smell, peering down through her glasses at Jamjar.

Jamjar explained everything that'd happened so far that day, all the way up to us searching for the THINGY on Planet Bin and meeting Professor Smell herself. 'You've obviously got a top notch shnozzle,' she said, pointing at the old lady's nostrils. 'Maybe you could sniff the THINGY out for us?'

'I don't know about that, Jamjar,' said Professor Smell. 'I've never even smelt a THINGY before - we always had toast for breakfast. I'm afraid I wouldn't know what I was sniffing for . . .'

Jamjar smiled. 'Not a problem,' she said. 'Just have a whiff of Mr X's brain - he had that THINGY stuck inside it practically his whole life. It's bound to still stink of it a bit!'

Professor Smell's nose drooped. 'You want me to smell that ugly little man's brains?' she gasped.

Mr X grinned up at her. 'Please, be my guest!' he said, giving his head a wobble, and the brain swished from side to side.

Professor Smell gulped. 'Well OK, I suppose it might be interesting,' she said, tiptoeing forward. 'But just this once.' She lowered her nostrils down towards Mr X's brain and breathed in gently.

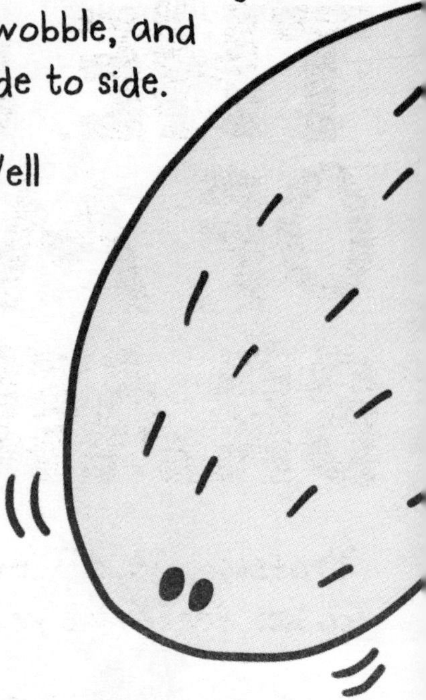

'Oh my goodness gracious me,' she warbled, staggering backwards and collapsing on to the floor.

THE SMELL OF MR X'S BRAIN

'Professor Smell!' cried Jamjar, helping her to her feet. 'Are you OK?'

Professor Smell blinked, dazedly. 'Never before have I sniffed such a wretched combination of odours,' she warbled.

'Why thank you!' smiled Mr X.

'WHAT ABOUT THE THINGY?' bleeped Wheelie. 'DID YOU GET A WHIFF OF IT, MADAM SMELL?'

'Hard to tell,' said Professor Smell. 'There was so much to take in . . .'

Jamjar pushed her glasses up her nose for the eight million and oneth time that morning. 'Try and remember if it was in there somewhere,' she said.

Professor Smell closed her eyes and waggled her nose. 'Hmm, let me think,' she said, as if she was re-smelling what she'd just smelled. 'There were lots of different cheeses - all the smelliest, stinkiest ones, of course.'

'Mmm, cheese - my favourite,' smiled Mr X.

'I didn't know brains smelt of cheese,' said Splorg.

'And dog poo,' said Professor Smell.

'DOG POO?' bleeped Wheelie. 'HOW IN THE LID-FLAPS COULD A BRAIN SMELL OF DOG POO?'

'Well I am always THINKING of dog poo,' grinned Mr X. 'I love it – it's so squidgy!'

Professor Smell twitched her nostrils some more. 'The aroma of rotten mushrooms was quite strong. Oh, and off milk.'

'Is anyone else's mouth watering?' said Mr X, beginning to drool.

'And then there was the smell of . . .' Professor Smell stopped talking and thought for a millisecond. 'Well, I've never really smelt anything like it.'

Mr X's eyes opened wide. 'Was it sort of like a spiky, cereal-y kind of whiff?' he said.

Professor Smell clicked her fingers with her eyes still closed. 'Exactly,' she said, pointing at Mr X. 'I couldn't have put it better myself!'

'That's the smell of THINGYS!' grinned Mr X.

SNUFFLING FOR THE THINGY

'Hurry, Professor Smell!' said Jamjar, guiding her over to the bit of Planet Bin where The Great Rubbish Chute had dumped us out. 'Get sniffing for that THINGY!'

Professor Smell, who still had her eyes closed, started to rummage her nose around like it was a hoover. 'Nothing but leaf socks here,' she said, snuffling frantically.

'Get that hooter of yours right in there, Professor Smell!' said Splorg, gently nudging the back of her head so that her nose dug right into the rubbish.

'I'm getting something!' said Professor Smell, digging her nose in deeper. 'Spiky . . . cereal-y . . . I think it might be a . . . WAAAHHH!!!'

Professor Smell whipped her shnozzle out of the rubbish and opened her eyes. 'HELLP!!! It's stuck to the end of my nose!' she wailed.

I Future-Ratboy-zoomed my eyes in on the end of Professor Smell's nose and spotted something familikeels stuck to the end of it.

'It's the THINGY!' I cried.

STUCK ON PLANET BIN

Wheelie grabbed the THINGY between his rubber-gloved fingers and plucked it off Professor Smell's nose. 'IT'S A CURIOUS LITTLE SPECIMEN,' he said, scratching his lid with his other hand.

Mr X peered up at the THINGY.
'We meet at last!' he smiled, licking his lips.

'Quick, slot it into Mr X's brain!' said Splorg.

'NO!' I screeched, sounding a bit like Not Bird.

'Ratboy's right,' said Jamjar. 'We don't want to turn him back into a baddy just yet - not until we've returned to Shnozville and located Gozo.'

And that's when we all realised something - The Great Rubbish Chute only sucked in one direction.

'We're stuck on Planet Bin!' cried Splorg, staring up at the spinning tennis ball in the sky. 'How in the unkeelness are we gonna get back to Earth?'

We stood there in silence for a few milliseconds, trying to think. Then Professor Smell clicked her fingers.

'I've got it,' she grinned. 'You can borrow my nose rocket!'

ATTACK OF THE SPACE HEDGEHOG

'It's just over here!' shouted Professor Smell, stomping through the rubbish towards a giant nose-shaped rocket I hadn't spotted before. 'Now, where did I put the key?'

She patted her rucksack, which had about seventeen pockets on the front of it, none of which seemed to have the nose rocket key inside them.

'No rush,' smiled Mr X, peering out to space. 'I'm just enjoying the view.'

'Don't listen to him,' said Jamjar. 'There's a giant vending machine monster eating his way through Shnozville with our best friends inside its belly – the sooner we get back and turn it off the better.'

Professor Smell stuck her hand into her dress pocket and waggled it around. 'I'll have you out of here in a jiffy,' she warbled, as a very loud snuffling sound snaked its way down my ratty earholes.

'What in the name of unkeelness was that noise?' I said, turning round and spotting a giant hedgehog trotting towards us.

'Oh cripes, we must've woken one of the Space Hedgehogs up with all our chatter,' said Professor Smell, opening up her rucksack and rummaging around inside.

Splorg's big blue head turned light turquoise. 'What do we do now?' he squeaked.

'I'll save you, gang!' cried Mr X, wobbling off towards the Space Hedgehog, waggling his hands in the air. 'Cooee, Mr Hedgehog! Eat my brains!'

Jamjar sprinted after Mr X and grabbed him by the hood. 'That's ever so nice of you Mr X, but I'm afraid we need you in one piece,' she said, dragging him back towards the nose rocket.

The Space Hedgehog stopped trotting and snuffled his snout into a pile of rubbish, scratching his front legs on the floor like a bull.

bleeped Wheelie.

'They tend to do that when they're about to charge,' muttered Professor Smell, whipping old crumpled-up tissues and half-full packets of chewing gum out of her bag. 'There it is!' she beamed, holding up the key.

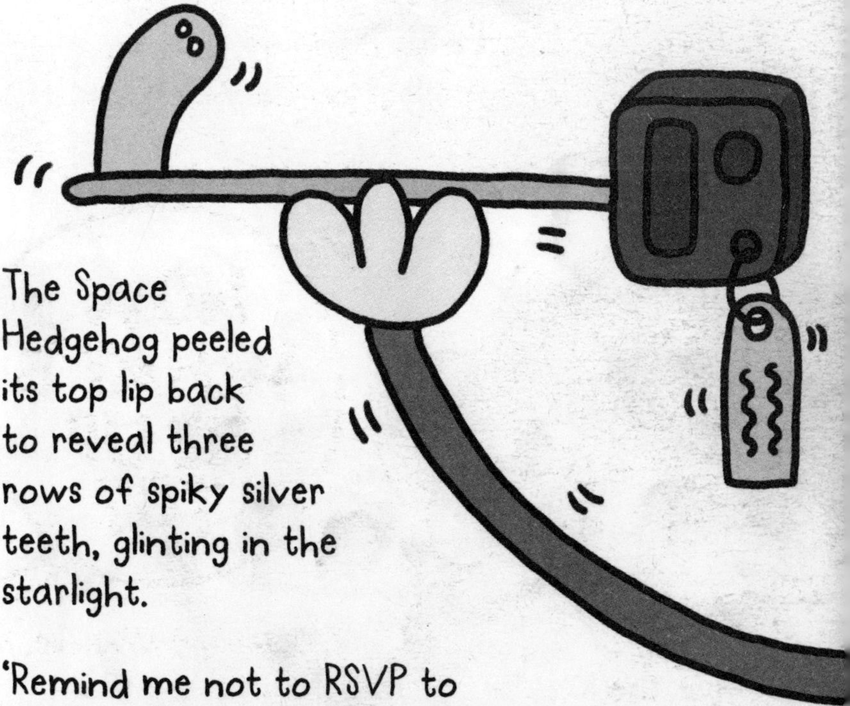

The Space Hedgehog peeled its top lip back to reveal three rows of spiky silver teeth, glinting in the starlight.

'Remind me not to RSVP to Mayor Goodhair's birthday party next year,' cried Splorg, grabbing the key out of Professor Smell's hand and clambering up a ladder to the door inside the nostrils of the nose rocket.

The Space Hedgehog let out a roar and started to charge. 'Get into that hooter, children,' wailed Professor Smell, lifting a trap door in the ground and jumping down into a little hole.

'Give the key to Dr Smell and ask him to drop the rocket back tomorrow. Tell him I'll make his favourite for tea!' she smiled, as the trap door slammed shut and Splorg started the engine.

ON THE WAY BACK

'That was WAY too close,' cried Splorg, as the nose rocket took off, the Space Hedgehog snapping at the bogie-shaped clouds of smoke puffing out of its exhaust pipe. 'Nose rocket, take us back to Shnozville!'

'OK, here's the plan,' said Jamjar. 'As soon as we get to Bunny Deli we'll shoot the THINGY into Mr X's brain and turn him back to bad.'

'There's only one problem,' I said. 'Once we turn Mr X back into a baddy he's not exactly going to want to help us out, is he?'

Mr X grinned. 'Just as well I happen to know a little secret about yours truly then, isn't it?'

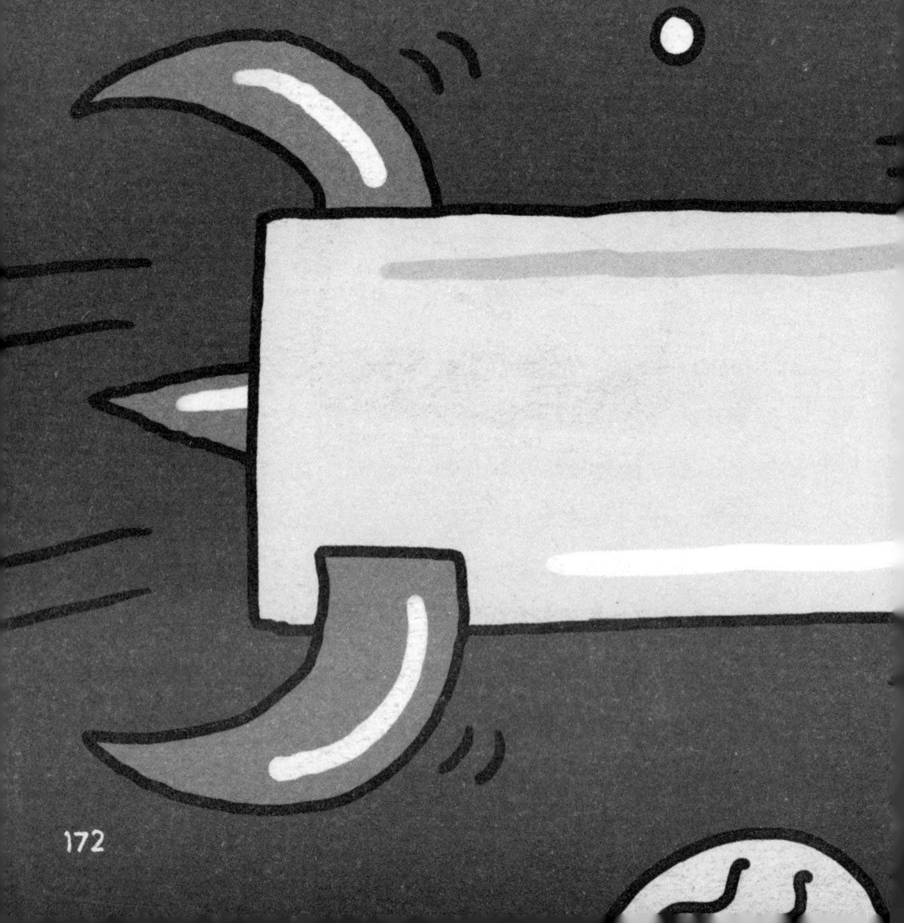

'What's the little secret?' asked Splorg.

'I'm ticklish!' whispered Mr X.

'SO?' bleeped Wheelie.

'So if you ever wanted to get me to do something I didn't want to do . . .'

'We tickle you until you give in!' laughed Jamjar, and Mr X nodded.

'I have to say,' said Splorg. 'I'm going to miss this new goody-goody version of Mr X.'

'Me too,' smiled Mr X, 'but we have to rescue your pals from that horrible great big beast before it eats the whole of Shnozville!'

'That's a point,' said Jamjar, whipping her Triangulator out of her pocket and pressing a button. 'Where IS Gozo?'

A beam shot out of the Triangulator and a hologram of Gozo appeared, stomping through Shnozville, popping a hover-lorry into his mouth like it was a chocolate bar.

'Looks like he's heading towards Bunny Deli – we'd better hurry,' said Splorg, pushing a lever, and the nose rocket jolted forwards even faster.

I straightened out my TV aerials and tried not to think about my mum and dad and little sister back in the olden days, hoping I'd show up for my birthday.

'What's on your mind, Ratboy?' said Jamjar, and I blinked.

'Nothing,' I said, as the nose rocket landed on the hover-pavement across the road from Bunny Deli.

BUNNY DELI

BACK IN SHNOZ-VILLE

'Ahh, Bunny Deli my old friend!' cried Splorg, glancing across the street. 'Is that a sight for sore eyeballs or what?'

I looked over at the little shop and smiled. Even though Bunny Deli wasn't my real home, it was nice to be back. I tilted my head up to the top of the building and spotted the giant plastic Cheesebleurgher Meal Deal that sat on its roof, wondering to myself why Gozo hadn't eaten that yet.

'Hello gang!' smiled Bunny as the doors whooshed open and we rushed in. Mayor Goodhair was standing behind her with mud splattered all over his face.

'What happened to you, old pal?' chuckled Mr X.

'He's not your pal, Mr X,' said Bunny. 'Not after everything he did to you.'

Mayor Goodhair sighed, patting Norman the hover-scissors, who was having another nap in his pocket. 'I've had a TERRIBLE morning,' he warbled. 'You do NOT want to mess with that monster, believe me!'

'Looks like you got a taste of your own medicine,' said Jamjar. 'Bunny, did you get that straw?'

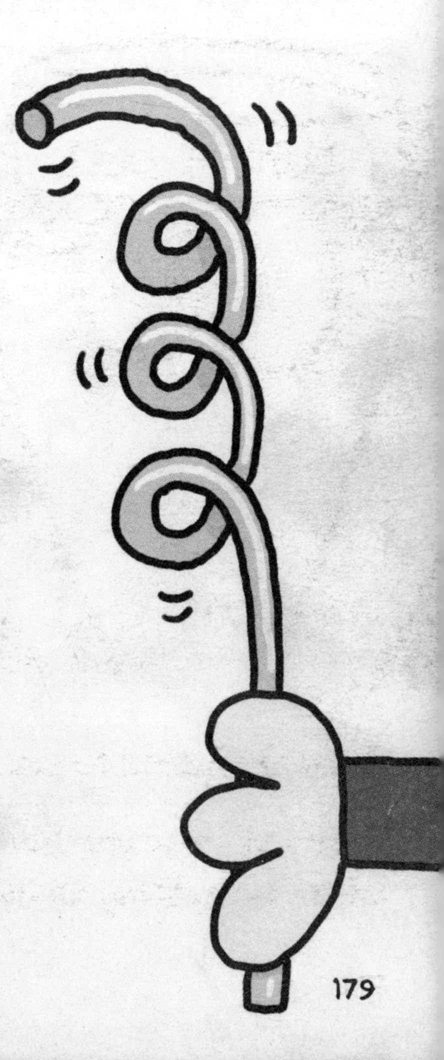

Bunny held up a curly pink straw. 'Will this do?' she smiled.

Jamjar grabbed the straw. 'Good work, Bunny,' she said. 'Now we just have to find Gozo and we can turn Mr X back to bad.'

Outside, the whole street went dark. 'What's going on?' I cried.

Splorg looked through the window and gasped. 'M-m-m-monster!!!' he wailed, as Gozo's head appeared from behind a skyscraper.

We all ran out on to the street and Gozo's three eyes blinked down at us. Every single shelf in his window belly was filled up with stuff from Shnozville now – all except for one slot.

I peered up at Twoface and Not Bird, trapped inside their plastic packet, and even though I was still in a bit of a bad mood with them, I felt my heart do a hiccup.

'Wheelie - the THINGY!' cried Jamjar.

Wheelie passed Jamjar the THINGY and she handed it and the straw to the mayor. 'Why don't you do the honours, Mayor Goodhair?' she said.

The mayor looked down at the straw and the THINGY. 'What in the name of two-in-one shampoo and conditioner is this all about?' he said.

Jamjar explained our plan.

'What, you want ME to . . .'

'Shoot the THINGY back into Mr X's brain?' said Jamjar. 'Got it in one, Mr Mayor!'

Mr X grinned at Mayor Goodhair. 'For old time's sake?' he said, pointing at his shiny pink thinker.

The mayor held the curly straw up to his mouth and slotted the THINGY in the end of it. 'Time to get my statue back,' he said, taking a deep breath.

The THINGY shot through the air like a tiny, spiky nose rocket towards Mr X's glistening brain.

'Been nice knowing you, gang!' smiled Mr X, blowing us all a stinky kiss as the THINGY struck the pink jelly-like globule with a thwunk and slowly sunk into it.

Mr X's eyebrows twizzled into their baddy positions and he blinked an evil blink. 'Ah, that's better,' he growled, looking up at his vending machine monster. 'Let's get the keelness out of here, Gozo!'

'QUICK, TICKLE HIM UNTIL HE TELLS US WHERE THAT HORRIBLE MUDDY BEAST'S OFF SWITCH IS,' bleeped Wheelie, pincering both of Mr X's arms with his rubber gloves.

'Here, tiggy tiggy!' sniggled Splorg, tiptoeing towards Mr X, his alien blue fingers waggling.

Mr X squirmed. 'No, not tickling!' he wailed. 'I'll tell you where the OFF switch is!'

'Well that was easier than I thought it'd be!' I chuckled, forward-rolling over to Mr X and giving him a quick tickle under the chin, just for old time's sake.

Which was maybe not such a keel idea after all.

'AH HA HA HA!' giggled Mr X, his mouth opening wide. 'HEE HEE HEE, NO, I CAN'T TAKE IT!' he wailed, and he began to breath in in strange little bursts.

'Stand back, he's going to blow!' cried Mayor Goodhair, as Mr X took one last little breath.

'A-CHOO!' he sneezed, and the THINGY flew out of his nostril, up into the air, did a loop-the-loop, then fell down into his mouth.

DISTANT RUMBLE

Mr X swallowed the THINGY in one. 'Cor, you're not kidding about how spiky those things are,' he said. 'Funny tasting too, aren't they!'

We all stood in silence, watching Mr X patting his tummy. 'Oops,' he grinned. 'I wasn't supposed to do that, was I?'

'Now what do we do?!' cried Mayor Goodhair, flapping his arms like a chicken. 'How are we supposed to turn Mr X back into a baddy if he's eaten the last blooming THINGY?'

Mr X blinked. 'I am SO sorry gang,' he said. 'Did I mention I start sneezing when people tickle me?'

Gozo roared, his mouth opening wide, and I peered up into his horrible face hole, spotting something weird-looking at the back of it.

'Is that . . . it can't be, can it?'

'WHAT IS IT, SHNOZVILLE SUPERHERO OF THE MONTH?' bleeped Wheelie, and I pointed into Gozo's mouth.

'It's Gozo's switch!' I cried.

GOZO'S SWITCH

The whole gang stared up into Gozo's mouth. There, at the back of his throat, was a switch. Except this switch didn't say ON/OFF on it. It said GOOD/BAD.

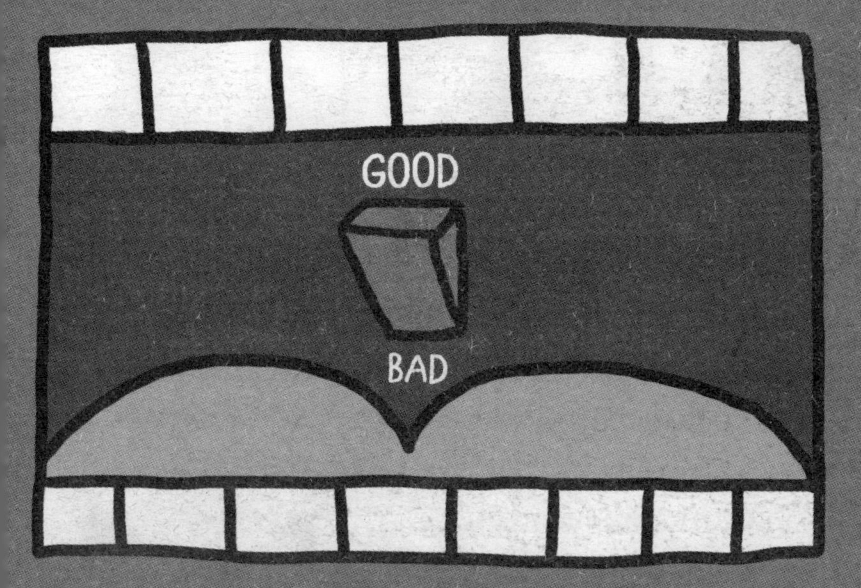

'That's weird,' I said. 'A GOOD/BAD switch.'

'Perhaps when I was designing Gozo I thought it'd be a bit of fun if you could turn him into a goody-goody now and then?' said Mr X.

'A bit like you!' chuckled Splorg.

Jamjar pointed her Triangulator up at Gozo's mouth. 'According to these readings, all we have to do is switch the monster to GOOD. Once we've done that it should be happy to help us with anything we need.'

'Then we'll be able to rescue Twoface and Not Bird!' smiled Splorg, looking all proud of himself for understanding what Jamjar had said.

'Oh this is just brilliant,' groaned the mayor, scratching his cap. 'How are we supposed to switch the blooming thing to GOOD without getting eaten ourselves?'

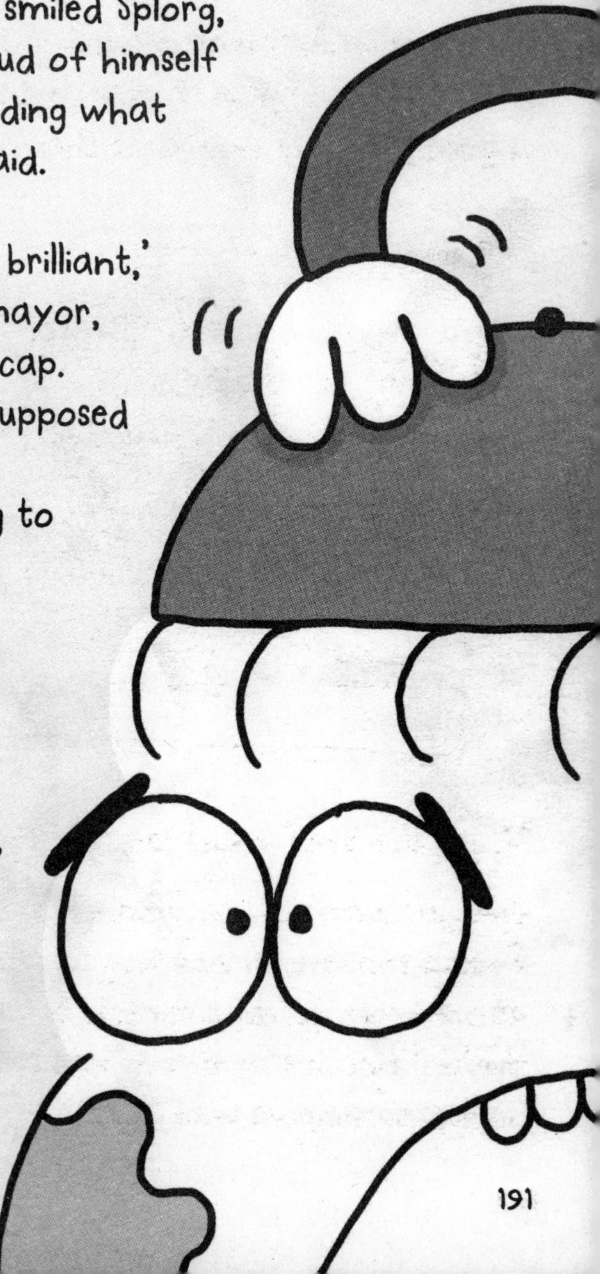

'Hmm, I think that must've been my plan!' giggled Mr X. 'Ooh, I was a horrible old meany, wasn't I!'

Gozo shut his mouth and reached down for the giant plastic Cheesebleurgher Meal Deal that was sitting on top of the Bunny Deli building.

'Sizzling hover-sausages – looks like Gozo's about to eat my Cheesebleurgher Meal Deal for his pudding!' cried Bunny.

Mayor Goodhair took his cap off, turned to Bunny and smiled a very unsmiley smile. 'Would you PLEASE put a sock in it, old lady,' he snapped. 'You are not helping me think.'

And that's when I came up with another one of my brilliant and amazekeel ideas.

'That's it!'

I cried, clicking my ratty fingers.

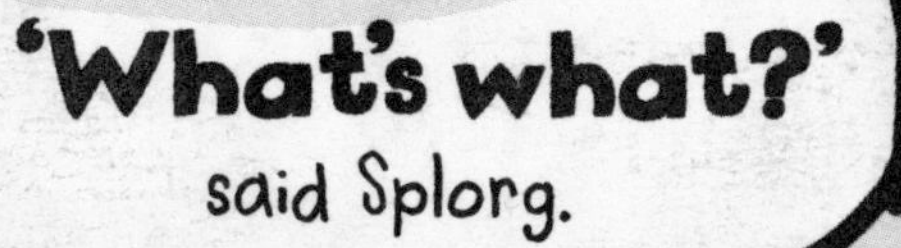

'Put a sock in it!'

I smiled.

'I'd expect that kind of language from Mayor Goodhair,' said Bunny, looking disappointed. 'But not you, Ratboy.'

'No, put a sock in Gozo's mouth,' I cried.

The whole gang, Gozo included, looked at me. 'WITH ALL DUE RESPECT, SIR, WHAT IN THE NAME OF UNKEELNESS ARE YOU RATTLING ON ABOUT?' bleeped Wheelie.

I pointed up at Gozo. He was holding the plastic Cheesebleurgher Meal Deal and opening his rectangle-shaped mouth wide. 'What's inside that mouth?' I asked.

'Gozo's switch!' everyone answered.

'And what do we want to do with it?' I cried.

'Turn it to GOOD!' they all shouted.

I pointed at the hover-pavement, covered in leaf socks.

'Then pick up a leaf sock and aim it at the switch!' I cried.

ACTUKEELY PUTTING A SOCK IN IT

Gozo moved the Cheesebleurgher Meal Deal closer to his mouth. 'PUD PUDS,' he boomed.

'Now!' I shouted, and Splorg threw a handful of leaf socks towards the giant face hole. The leaf socks flew through the air like, erm . . . socks, and landed in Gozo's mouth.

'Close!' I cried, but the switch was still pointing to BAD.

'UNGF!' said Gozo, plonking the Meal Deal back on top of the skyscraper and putting his hand up to his mouth. 'YUCK!' he boomed, spitting out a giant globule of chewed-up leaf socks.

The big ball of sock spit hurtled down through the sky and landed splat on top of Mayor Goodhair's head.

'Waaah, my hair!' he cried.

'More! Throw more!' I shouted, scooping up another handful of leaf socks and throwing them into Gozo's mouth.

'GAAA!!!' groaned Gozo, his mouth filling up with leaf socks.

'Aim for the switch!' I cried.

'That's what we're trying to do!' shouted Jamjar.

Mr X grabbed an armful and starting to throw too. 'This is fun!' he giggled.

You know when you're watching one of those films where everyone's throwing handfuls of leaf socks into a giant monster's mouth, trying to turn a switch to GOOD at the back of it? That's what was happening now.

'One more leaf sock left,' said Jamjar, passing it to me. 'This is a job for Shnozville Superhero of the Month.'

I took the sock and smiled at Jamjar. 'Here goes!' I said, Future-Ratboy-zooming my eyes in on the switch and pulling my arm back.

'By the power of playing it keel times a millikeels!' I cried, as I shot my arm forward and let go of the leaf sock.

The leaf sock flew through the air like a, erm . . . sock, and straight into Gozo's mouth.

'Good throw!' cheered Mr X, as I closed my eyes and crossed my ratty fingers.

For a millisecond, all I could hear was the rustle of leaf socks in the trees.

And then there was a click.

I opened my eyes and peered up at Gozo. His three gigantic eyes blinked one after the other, and he opened his mouth.

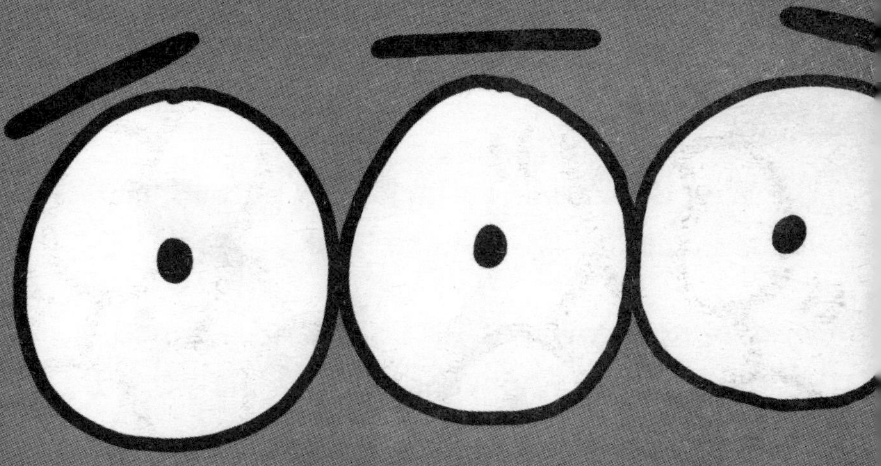

'Goodness me, you would not believe the nightmare I've just had!' he chimed.

RETURN OF THE WISE OLD VENDING MACHINE

'That voice,' I said. 'It's very familikeels.'

'Ratboy, is that you?' chimed Gozo, smiling down at me.

'The Wise Old Vending Machine!' I gasped, realising whose voice it was. 'You're back . . . sort of!'

Gozo looked down at his body and jumped. 'Waahh, what's happened to me?' he yelped.

'Mr X over there made a few alterations,' grumbled Mayor Goodhair, scraping leaf sock gunk out of his hair.

'We can explain everything later, Wise Old Vending Machine,' said Jamjar. 'First let's get Twoface and Not Bird out of you!'

Splorg looked up at The Wise Old Vending Machine's window belly.

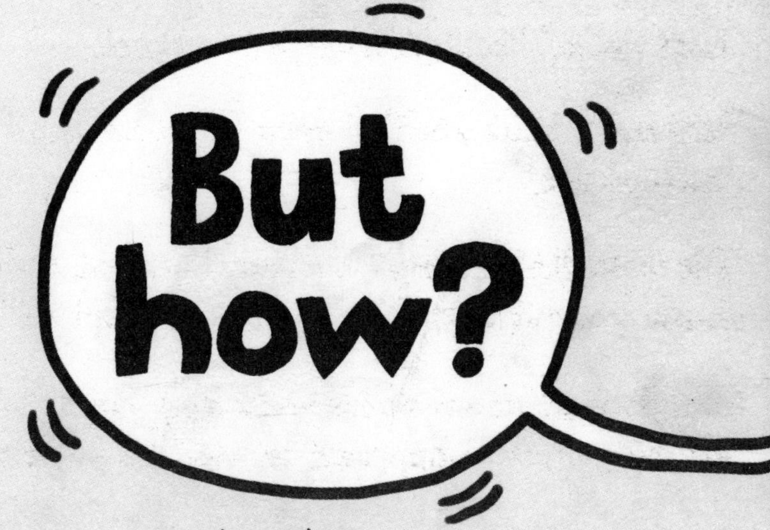

he asked.

'Good question Splorg,' said the mayor. 'Smash the window or something?'

We all gasped. 'You can't smash The Wise Old Vending Machine's window!' I cried.

Jamjar pointed her Triangulator at the monster's window belly. 'That plastic is triple polymer. It's got a reinforced platinum frame. Mr X sealed it with top-notch epoxy resin,' she said.

We all turned to Jamjar and did our confused faces. 'What I'm saying is, we're never going to get through that window,' she said.

'Sorry, gang!' smiled Mr X, looking guilty.

'So this was your plan?' said Mayor Goodhair. 'To turn Gozo into The Wise Old Vending Machine then stand around scratching your bums, trying to work out what to do next?'

Jamjar nodded, sadly. 'It's true, we didn't exactly think it through properly,' she said. 'I blame myself completely.'

'Ooh, don't be so hard on yourself, Jamjar,' said Bunny, giving her a little cuddle. 'You're a very clever young lady!'

'Thanks Bunny,' said Jamjar. 'Wise Old Vending Machine, can you help?'

'I'm sorry Jamjar,' chimed The Wise Old Vending Machine, 'but the only way you're going to get Twoface and Not Bird out of my belly is if you can magic up a giant coin.'

He pointed up at the humungous coin slot next to his window belly.

'Come on, Mr X,' said Mayor Goodhair, his hair sticking out in all directions with leaf sock gunk. 'You built this whole stupid monster all on your own. Surely you can knock up an oversized coin to fit its slot?'

Mr X grinned and knocked on his brain, like it was a front door. 'I'd love to help you, really I would,' he said. 'But I just don't have the baddy-power for that sort of thing any more.'

We looked at the monster, standing there in the middle of the road outside Bunny Deli, his belly filled with stuff. A line of hover-cars stretched down the street in both directions, beeping their horns.

'Some birthday this turned out to be,' said Mayor Goodhair, looking down at his feet. He was standing on one of his Mayor Goodhair manhole covers. 'At least old Gozo didn't eat any of my new manhole covers I spose,' he said.

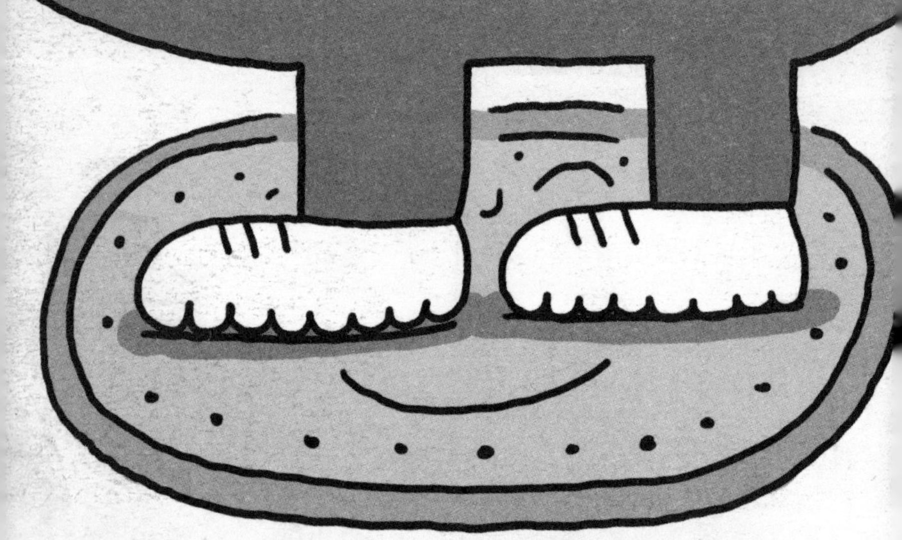

And that's when I had ANOTHER one of my brilliant and amazekeel ideas. I glanced up at the coin slot next to the monster's window belly, then down at the Mayor Goodhair manhole cover. 'I know how to get your statues back!' I cried.

HOW TO GET THE STATUES BACK

'What do you mean, Ratboy?' asked Bunny.

'Two words,'

I said, and they all went quiet, waiting to hear my two words.

'Manhole covers?' asked Splorg, once I'd said my two words.

'Manhole covers!' I grinned. 'They're exakeely the right size for that coin slot!'

Everyone looked up at the coin slot next to Gozo's window belly.

'Hey, you're right,' smiled Jamjar.

'Wait a billisecond,' said Mayor Goodhair. 'I'm not having you going around lifting up all my brand new manhole covers!'

He plonked his fat bum down on top of the one he'd been standing on and crossed his arms.

'Don't worry, Mayor Goodhair,' I said, starting to run all the way back to Shnozville Dump.

'OOH, IT IS GOOD TO BE BACK HERE AGAIN!' bleeped Wheelie as we arrived at the gates to Shnozville Dump. 'WHAT ARE WE DOING HERE EXACTLY, SIR?'

I pointed at the row of old manhole covers with the 'HELP YOURSELF!' sign rested up in front of them.

'Help yourself?' chuckled Splorg. 'Who'd want to help themselves to a boring old manhole cov . . . OHH, I get it.'

I said.

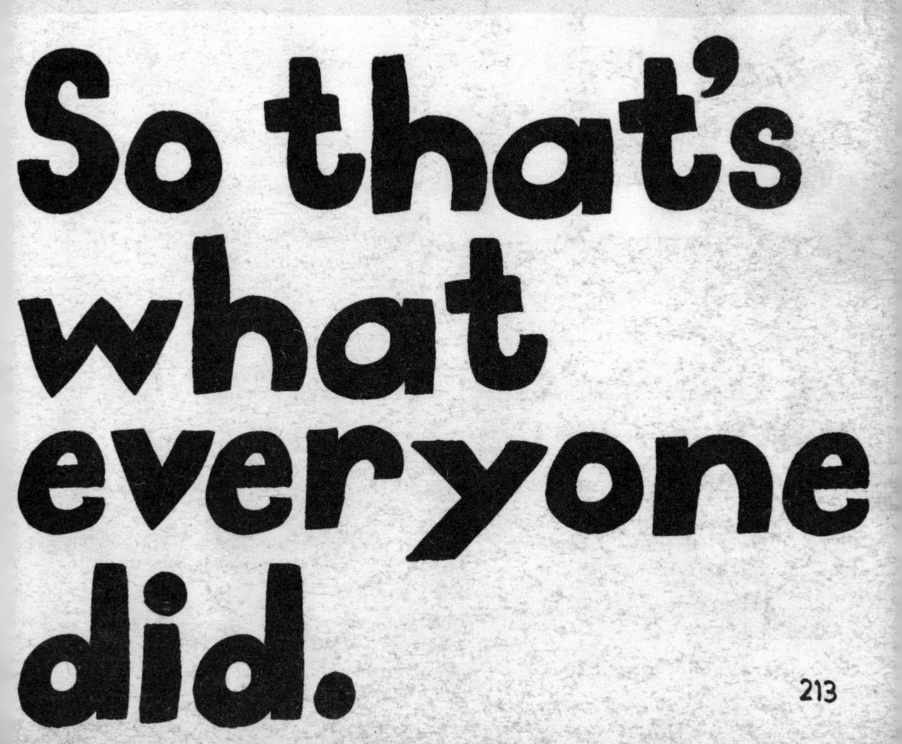

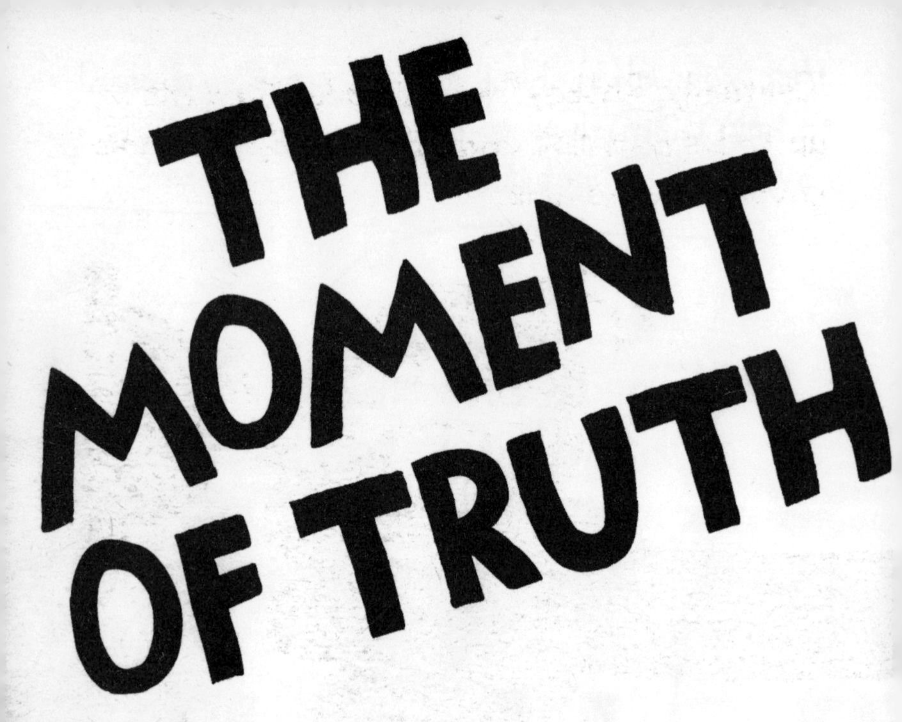

THE MOMENT OF TRUTH

You know how you'd expect a manhole cover to be really heavy? Well these ones were hover-manhole covers, so they weren't heavy at all.

'Give me a hand would you, Wise Old Vending Machine?' I said, jumping into his palm once we'd got back to Bunny Deli, all of us carrying about seventeen hover-manhole covers each.

'Certainly, Ratboy!' he chimed, lifting me up to his coin slot and I pushed my manhole cover into the hole.

'Perfect fit!' I cried, giving the gang a thumbs-up.

'Now press the button for my statue!' ordered Mayor Goodhair, but I just ignored him.

The Wise Old Vending Machine lowered me to his giant buttons and I pressed the third one down.

A robot metal arm whirred to life inside his belly, grabbed the Twoface and Not Bird package off the top shelf, and dumped it into the tray underneath.

'It worked!' cried Splorg, pushing open the hatch under the monster's window belly and reaching in. 'Give me a hand, Wheelie,' he said, and Wheelie coiled his arm round the package and pulled it out.

'Ooh Ratboy, you are a clever clogs,' grinned Bunny. 'Now, let's get those two out of that packet!'

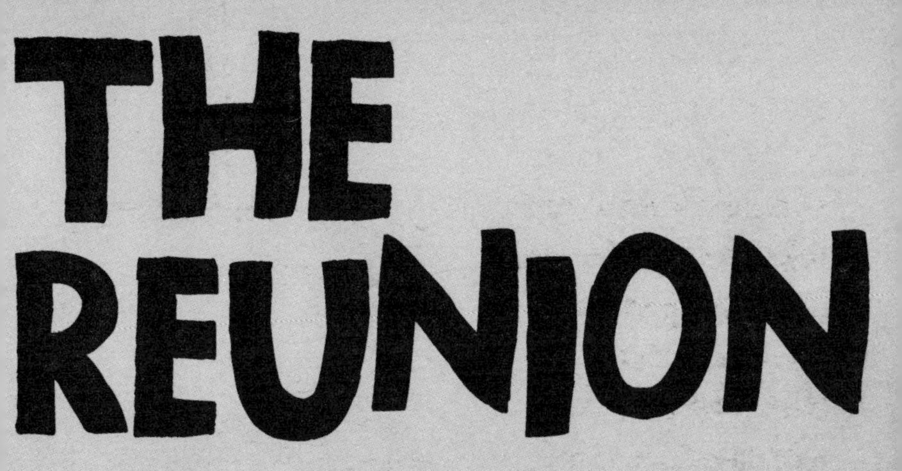

'Air! I need air!' gasped Twoface as we ripped the plastic open and dragged him out of his mould.

'NOT!' squawked Not Bird, zooming out of the packet and fluttering over to my shoulder.

'Don't you "NOT!" me, you stupid little fluff ball!' said Twoface. He turned to me. 'I don't know how you put up with him, Ratboy.'

'Sounds like you two have been having fun!' giggled Splorg, patting Twoface on the back.

'Ugh, you don't even want to know,' groaned Twoface. 'He never stopped fidgeting the whole time!'

'NOT!' screeched Not Bird, right into my ear, and my ratty little ear hairs vibrated, making me sniggle.

'So you're both OK then are you?' asked Bunny, giving them a hug each.

Twoface peered down at his costume. 'Looks like I'm still all here,' he said.

'NOT!' squawked Not Bird again, nuzzling his furry little face into my neck.

'Stop it, Not Bird!' I giggled. 'That tickles!'

'Ahh, isn't that lovely,' cooed Mr X, and Twoface did his confused faces.

'Eh?' he jumped, stepping backwards. 'What in the name of unkeelness is HE doing here?'

'I'll explain later,' smiled Jamjar, putting one of her arms round Mr X and another round Twoface. And seeing as she still had three arms left, she put them round me, Splorg and Bunny too.

Mayor Goodhair pulled his phone out and pointed it in our direction. 'Say "KEEL!"' he said, and we all smiled as he snapped a photo of the keelest gang of weirdos the future has ever seen.

GROUP NOT!

It was eighteen minutes and four hundred and seventy two seconds later and Jamjar had explained everything to Twoface and Not Bird.

'Can somebody PLEASE move that monster out of the road?!' cried a man in a hover-car, beeping his horn, and The Wise Old Vending Machine gave him a wave.

'I do apologise!' he chimed, taking a step over to the hover-pavement next to Bunny Deli. 'There. Not a bad spot,' he said, plonking his bum down. 'I think I might set up shop right here!'

Bunny crossed her arms, frowning at The Wise Old Vending Machine, and I smiled a sad smile.

'I'm really going to miss you lot,' I said, and the whole gang stopped what they were doing and looked at me.

'What did you just say?' said Twoface, and I looked down, trying to work out how to explain it.

'Well,' I said, 'I don't know if anyone's noticed, but I sort of . . . don't exactly . . . need to be here any more . . .'

Bunny tilted her eyebrows. 'What in the blazes are you blathering on about, Ratboy?' she asked.

I pointed at Mr X. 'Anyone remember what I promised I'd do once we finally defeated Mr X?' I asked.

Splorg shot his hand up. 'Ooh, ooh, I know!' he said. 'You said you'd zap yourself back to the olden days!'

Then he put his hand down again, as he realised something.

'Oh . . . no – wait!' he said. 'But you HAVEN'T defeated Mr X – he's still standing right over there!'

'That's true,' I said. 'But he's not exactly causing any trouble, is he?'

Everybody looked over at Mr X. He was helping Mayor Goodhair drag his birthday statue out of Gozo's hatch.

'So that's that. I can go home now,' I said.

Everyone went quiet. Then Jamjar opened her mouth.

she shouted, and my superhero eyebrows shot up my ratty forehead.

'What did you just say?' I said, copying what Twoface had said eight quadruple-seconds earlier.

'I won't let you go, Ratboy!' said Jamjar, a tear zigzagging down her cheek.

Splorg stepped forward.

he shouted.

Then Bunny opened her mouth.

she boomed too.

giggled Mr X, joining in.

'NOT!'

cried Twoface, wandering over next to me.

He put his hand on my shoulder. 'You're not going home because of me, are you?' he asked.

'No . . .' I said, ruffling the wings on his superhero hood. 'Well, maybe a little bit!'

squawked Not Bird, and we all sniggled.

'I don't want to leave you lot – really I don't,' I said. 'I just miss my mum and dad.'

I turned to Not Bird. 'Not Bird, you don't have to come if you don't want to. Or you, Wheelie - I know you both love it here.'

'BUT HOW WILL YOU ZAP YOURSELF BACK WITHOUT ME, SIR?' bleeped Wheelie.

'I thought I could use a hover-bin bag?' I said.

'NO MASTER OF MINE IS TRAVELLING THROUGH TIME IN A SEE-THROUGH PLASTIC HOVER-BIN BAG,' bleeped Wheelie.

'NOT!' squawked Not Bird, even though I knew he meant the opposite.

Jamjar tapped her Triangulator. 'There's a storm due next Flursday,' she said, sadly.

I put my arm round her. 'Well then, we'd better make the most of my last week then, hadn't we?' I said, my goggles filling up with ratty tears.

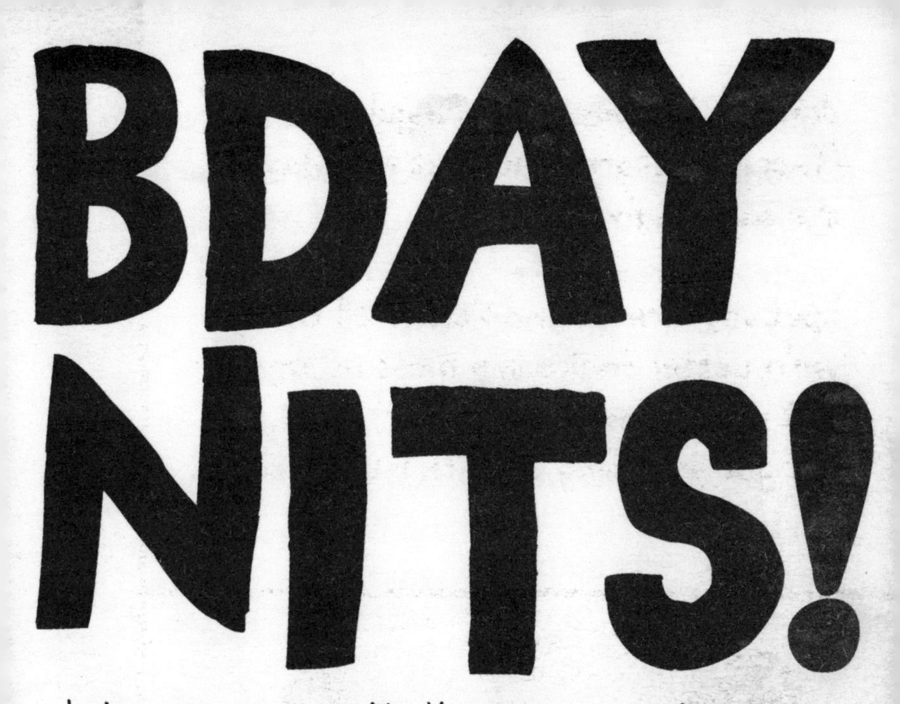

I glanced over at Mr X, who was smiling back at us all with a tear in his eye. 'It almost makes me want to turn back into a baddy,' he said. 'I hate to break you guys up!'

Not Bird fluttered over to him and landed on his brain, nestling down like a real-life wig.

'Don't you still want to get back at Mayor Goodhair a tiny bit, Mr X?' asked Splorg. 'I mean, he did steal your bowl of THINGYS every morning for your WHOLE childhood. That's a lot of breakfasts!'

'Nah,' said Mr X, looking over at Mayor Goodhair, who was standing next to his birthday statue, checking it for scratches. 'I think I've caused him enough trouble for one day!'

'Hey, that's a point,' said Twoface. 'How's the mayor gonna get that statue all the way back to Shnozville Town Square?'

Mayor Goodhair smiled. 'Don't you know who I am?' he said. 'I'll have this thing back in place in no time!'

He scratched his head again. 'First things first though, I need a hover-shower. I've got to get this leaf sock gunk out of my hair!'

Jamjar pulled the Triangulator out of her pocket and pointed it at the mayor's hair. 'Hmmm,' she said, smiling to herself. 'I'm not sure that's going to cut it . . .'

'What in the unkeelness are you taking about?' asked the mayor.

'The cross-pollination of those frondal perambulators with the behemoth's portal sputum has created an abiding epoxification,'

grinned Jamjar.

said Bunny.

'The mix of those chewed-up leaf socks and Gozo's spit has created a sort of gluey cement – it'll never wash out,' chuckled Jamjar.

'S-so what am I supposed to do now?' stuttered Mayor Goodhair, patting his gloopy barnet.

Jamjar pressed a button on her Triangulator. 'There's good news and there's bad news,' she said.

'What's the good news?' asked the mayor.

Jamjar pushed her glasses up her nose. 'The good news is that your hair will grow back,' she said.

'I don't think I want to hear the bad news . . .' whimpered Mayor Goodhair, as Norman peeked out of his trouser pocket.

Jamjar smiled at Norman. 'You know what to do, Norm!' she smiled, and he blinked, then floated out of the pocket, up to his owner's hair.

'Been anywhere nice on your holidays?' he squeaked, swishing his blades open.

'NOOOO!!!!' cried Mayor Goodhair, as Norman started to chop.

It was Flursday night and I was outside Bunny Deli, standing inside Wheelie with Not Bird tucked under my arm. Leaf socks swayed in the wind and multicoloured raindrops pitter-pattered on to my goggles.

'Say hello to your mum from me!' shouted Bunny over the crackle of thunder, and I gave her a thumbs-up.

Splorg and Twoface smiled sadly, as Jamjar pointed her Triangulator at Wheelie. 'Don't forget to use the Memoriser 350 as soon as you see your family!' she cried, her hair blowing across her face.

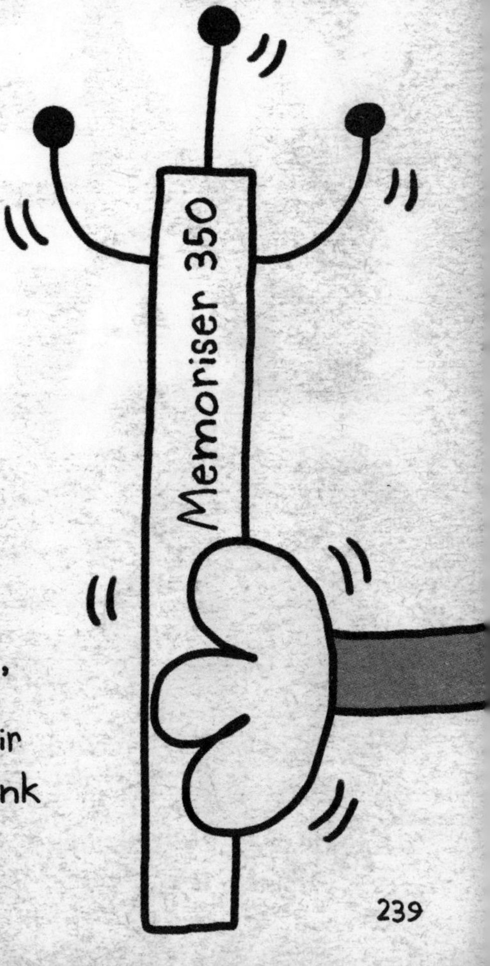

I held up the little gizmo she'd just given me. It was a see-through plastic stick with three prongs sticking out the end of it. 'Point it at their foreheads and press the button,' she said. 'It'll wipe their memories – they'll think you'd just popped down the shops!'

'NOT!' squawked Not Bird, and I patted his furry little head.

'There, there, Not Bird,' I said. 'Everything'll be OK.'

Wheelie flapped his lid, banging my head by accident. 'MAY I TAKE THIS OPPORTUNITY TO SAY FAREWELL, SIR?' he bleeped.

'But you're coming with me!' I shouted over the storm.

'THIS IS TRUE,' bleeped Wheelie. 'BUT I WON'T BE QUITE THE SAME AFTER OUR JOURNEY.'

A white line zigzagged across the sky.

'AS MADAM JAMJAR EXPLAINED, WE'LL BE ZAPPED BACK TO OUR ORIGINAL SELVES BY THE LIGHTNING,' he bleeped.

I gripped one of Wheelie's rubber gloves and looked him in the bit of his lid where his eyes would be if he had any. 'This is your last chance, Wheelie,' I said. 'You can back out now and I won't mind – I promise!'

'NONSENSE!' bleeped Wheelie, and Not Bird squawked 'NOT!'

I peered through the rain at the gang, huddled outside Bunny Deli under its hover-awning. Splorg's blue head glistened and Twoface was smiling with both his mouths. Bunny was waving all ten of her hands while Jamjar was still fiddling with her Triangulator.

She pushed her glasses up her nose one last time. 'Ratboy!' she cried. 'According to my calculations, there should be a bolt of lightning any . . .'

EVERY
THING
WENT
DARK.

I opened my eyes. 'What happened?' I said.

I realised I was sitting down, so I stood up.

'OW!' I said, bashing my head on the inside of Wheelie's lid. 'Sorry Wheelie.'

Nothing.

I flipped the lid open. I was back in my front garden – the one from the olden days. The sun was in the sky and a bird cheeped up in the branches of our little apple tree.

'It worked!' I cried. 'The lightning zapped us home, Not Bird!'

Nothing again.

I glanced down into the bin and spotted Not Bird, lying by my feet.

But Not Bird wasn't Not Bird any more - he was just a cuddly toy bird.

I looked up in the sky. No hover-cars were flying past, and the buildings next to my house weren't ginormous skyscrapers, they were just boring old normal houses like mine.

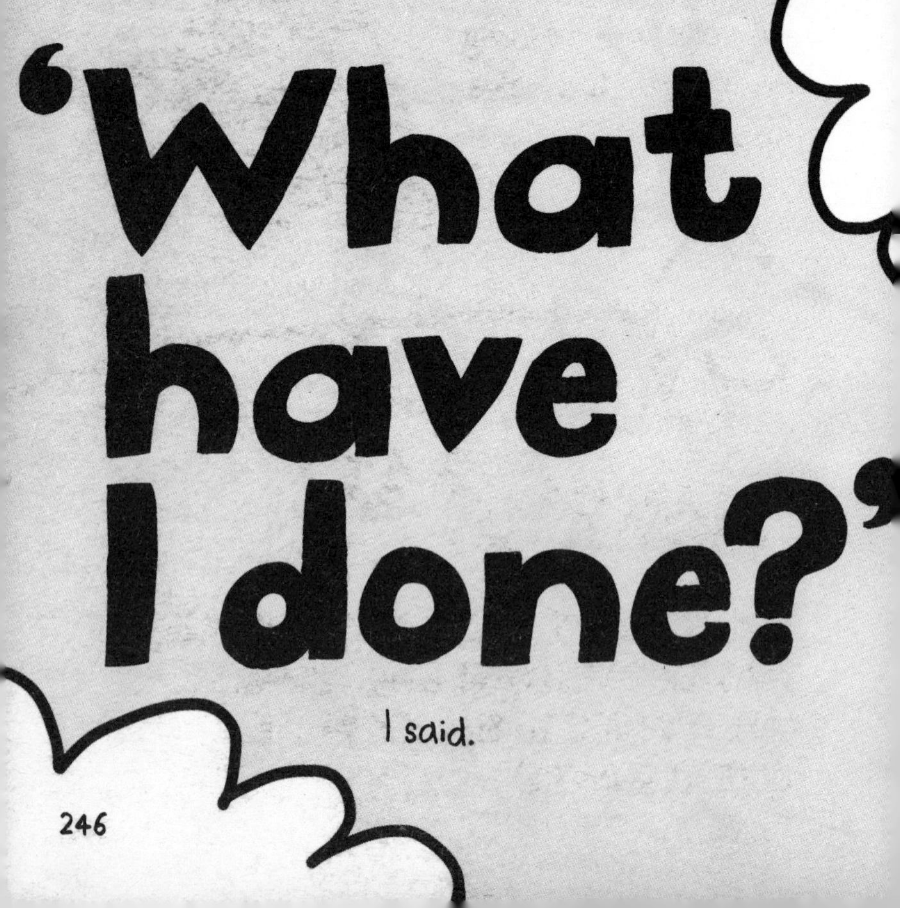

'What have I done?'

I said.

squawked Not Bird, fluttering out of Wheelie and landing on a branch of the apple tree.

'Huh?' I said.

'EVERYTHING'S SHIP SHAPE OVER HERE, MASTER RATBOY!' bleeped Wheelie. 'AH, IT'S NICE TO BE BACK IN THE GOOD OLD DAYS!'

'But Jamjar said you'd be zapped back to normal!' I cried, pinching the end of my nose to stop Wheelie's bin breath wafting up my nostrils.

And that's when I noticed something strange. 'Duh, dat's deird,' I said. 'Dy dose dill das a dlack dlob don de dend dof dit.'

'EXCUSE ME, SIR?' bleeped Wheelie. 'WOULD YOU MIND REMOVING YOUR FINGERS FROM THAT HOOTER OF YOURS SO I CAN UNDERSTAND WHAT YOU ARE ON ABOUT A LITTLE BETTER?'

I de-pinched my sniffer. 'My nose still has a black blob on the end of it,' I cried, patting the rest of my shnozzle. 'Waaahhh! It's still all hairy!'

Wheelie did a twirl on the spot. 'WELL, WELL, LOOKS LIKE MADAM JAMJAR'S CALCULATIONS WERE INCORRECT!' he bleeped. 'WE'VE BEEN ZAPPED BACK TO THE PAST, ALRIGHT - BUT AS OUR FUTURE SELVES!'

'This can't happen!' I cried. 'I'm sposed to be Colin Lamppost . . . what're my mum and dad gonna think when a half boy, half rat, half TV turns up on their doorstep? I don't think the Memoriser 350 is designed to deal with that!'

'C-colin?' wailed a familikeels voice. 'Is that really you, my darling?' wailed a familikeels voice.

'Oh my unkeelness, it's my mum!' I said, twizzling round at super-Future-Rat-speed so she couldn't see my face, and a shiny piece of paper fluttered out of my pocket, on to the grass.

I bent down and picked it up, flipped it over and looked at the faces smiling out at me.

'Now what do I do?' I said to the photo of Twoface, Splorg, Jamjar and Bunny.

Which was a stupid thing to do, because everyone knows photos can't answer questions.

And that was when the weirdest thing of all happened.

'Did you see that?' I gasped.

'SEE WHAT, SIR?' bleeped Wheelie.

'Jamjar's eye,' I said. 'It just winked!'

'NOT!' squawked Not Bird, but I just ignored him and carried on staring at the photo.

'Jamjar, is that you?' I whispered, and she waved, then Splorg waved too. And Bunny and Twoface three.

'Happy birthday, Ratboy!' they all called, and I lifted the photo up to my lips and gave it a great big ratty kiss.

'Thanks, keel-dudes!' I grinned. 'Who cares what I look like when I've got you lot as my friends!'

I stuffed the photo into my pocket and turned round to face the future. 'Mum, Dad, I'm home!' I cried, forward-rolling towards it.

THE END!

ABOUT THE AUTHOR

Jim Smith is the keelest kids' book author in the whole world amen.

He graduated from art school with first class honours (the best you can get) and went on to create the branding for a sweet little chain of coffee shops.

He also designs cards and gifts under the name Waldo Pancake. And removes his nose and eyeballs every evening before bed.